RALPH 124C 41+

by Hugo Gernsback

FOREWORDS BY DR. LEE DE FOREST AND FLETCHER PRATT

Martino Publishing
Mansfield Centre, CT
2014

Martino Publishing
P.O. Box 373,
Mansfield Centre, CT 06250 USA

ISBN   978-1-61427-577-0

© *2014 Martino Publishing*

Cover design by T. Matarazzo

Printed in the United States of America On 100% Acid-Free Paper

RALPH 124C 41+

by Hugo Gernsback

FOREWORDS BY DR. LEE DE FOREST AND FLETCHER PRATT

NEW YORK: FREDERICK FELL, INC.

CONTENTS

PREFACE

TO THE SECOND EDITION

SINCE the first edition of *Ralph 124C 41 +* in 1925, an eventful quarter century has passed. Since I first wrote the story, 39 amazing years have been swallowed into the Einstein space-time-continuum—years pregnant with scientific progress.

Since 1925, the 5,000-edition volume has had a rather remarkable career. It has been quoted by hundreds of authorities both great and small, in hundreds of publications —not only in the United States but also in many other countries. Whenever a history of science-fiction was written, *Ralph* nearly always was included routinely, much to my surprise.

In the meanwhile the book became a sort of museum piece. Early in 1950 the quoted price in the second-hand book market was $50.00 for a single copy. Left with only two copies of the 1925 edition I myself endeavored to buy a copy for a friend in France, but no copies were forthcoming even at $50.00!

Authors avowedly never read their own books—I am no exception to that rule. So the other day when I was reading proofs for the 1950 edition, after a lapse of 25 years, I began to ask myself a lot of questions.

Why for instance was *Ralph* written, in the first place?

In 1911 I was a young publisher—not yet 27 years old.

I had started publishing *Modern Electrics* in 1908, three years before. It was the world's *first* radio magazine. By 1911 it had attained a print order of around 100,000 copies and was for sale on all the principal newsstands in the U. S. and Canada, and sold by subscription all over the world.

Yet, today I must confess I do not recall just *what* prompted me to write *Ralph*. I do recall that I had no plan whatsoever for the whole of the story. I had no idea how it would end nor what the contents would be.

The story began in the April, 1911, issue of *Modern Electrics* and ended with the March, 1912, number. On the twelve covers of the magazine for that year there was a monthly illustration depicting some *Ralph* exploit as divulged in the current installment. Thus for instance the first (April, 1911) cover showed Ralph at the *Telephot*— not the broadcast television of today but person-to-person television by phone, which has as yet to be realized. (See illustration.)

Indeed the word *television* was practically unknown in 1911. (The first technical article in print, using the term, was written by me: "Television and the Telephot," *Modern Electrics*, December, 1909.

As the story developed from month to month there was the age-old scramble to beat the deadline—but somehow or other I always made it—usually under duress, finishing the installment at 3 or 4 A.M. on the last day. That the literary quality suffered painfully under such continuous *tours de force* every month, there can be no question, but somehow the scientific and technical content came through unscathed most of the time.

After 39 years I could point out a number of minor

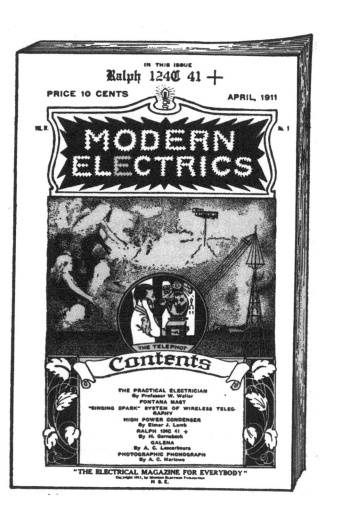

IN THIS ISSUE

Ralph 124C 41 +

PRICE 10 CENTS   **APRIL, 1911**

VOL. IV.   No. 1

MODERN ELECTRICS

THE TELEPHOT

Contents

"THE ELECTRICAL MAGAZINE FOR EVERYBODY"

technical flaws in some of my early predictions, but on the whole I probably could not do much better today. To be sure, I would not think of a gyroscopic propelled space flyer now, but then in 1911 no one was thinking of rocket-propelled or atomic-powered space flyers. In 1911 too, scientists still thought of a universal ether permeating all space. Today we seem to get along very well without it.

While quite a number of the scientific predictions made in *Ralph* have come to pass, many more are still unrealized. I have, however, little concern that all—or most of them—will come about in the not too distant future. I am certain that *all* of them will be commonplace by 2660, the time in which the action of this novel moves.

Perhaps I can do no better than reprint the foreword of the original 1911 *"Ralph"*:

This story which plays in the year 2660, will run serially during the coming year in MODERN ELECTRICS. It is intended to give the reader as accurate a prophecy of the future as is consistent with the present marvelous growth of science. The author wishes to call especial attention to the fact that while there may be extremely strange and improbable devices and scenes in this narrative, they are not impossible, or outside of the reach of science.

We are now at the beginning of a new and fantastic era —the electronic-atomic age—an age that makes the impossible come true overnight. If *Ralph 124C 41 +* can fire the present-day young minds with the same enthusiasm for scientific research and accomplishment as it did their fathers in the past, I shall feel amply repaid in having instigated this new, 1950 edition of *Ralph*.

HUGO GERNSBACK

New York, May 1950

PREFACE

TO THE FIRST EDITION

RALPH 124C 41 + first appeared as a serial in the author's first magazine, "Modern Electrics," in 1911. This magazine was first devoted exclusively to radio activities. At the time the story was written the word "radio" had not yet come into use. We were at that time still using the term "wireless."

It has been necessary, in view of scientific progress since the time the story was first written, and in order to present the book to a much wider reading public, to rewrite much of the story and to make many changes. Yet, the ideas and conceptions embodied in the original manuscript have been little altered.

The author appreciates that many of the predictions and statements appear to verge upon the fantastic. So was Jules Verne's submarine "Nautilus" in his famous story "Twenty Thousand Leagues Under the Sea." Verne's conception of the submarine was declared utterly ridiculous. Nevertheless, the prophecy was fulfilled. In fact, Verne's imagination hit far below the mark in what was actually accomplished by science since the book was written.

Lest you think that the author has gone too far into the realms of pure imagination, place yourself in the position of your great-great-grandfather being told about locomotives, steamships, X-rays, telegraphs, telephones, phonographs, electric lights, radio broadcasting, and the hundred other commonplaces of our lives today. Would he not have condemned such predictions as the height of folly and absurdity?

So with you. You are in the same position with respect to the prophecies in this work as your remote ancestor. Your descendants, picking up this book 750 years hence, —or at the time in which this story is laid,—will ridicule the author for his lack of imagination in conceiving the obvious developments in the first half of the next century.

It may be of passing interest to note that several of the predictions made by the author when this story was written have already become verities. Notable among these is what the author termed the *Hypnobioscope*, the purpose of which is to acquire knowledge while asleep. The author was greatly astonished to read the results obtained by J. A. Phinney, Chief Radioman, U. S. Navy, who, having tried the system himself, in 1923, introduced it at the Pensacola, Florida, Naval Training School. Here one may see naval students stretched out on long benches asleep with casket-like coverings over their heads. The caskets contain two telephone receivers through which radio code is sent to the sleeper. It has been demonstrated that the sleeping student can be taught code faster than by any other means, for the sub-conscious self never sleeps. Students who have failed in their studies have passed examinations after being taught by this method.

The scientific conception or vision of the world of 750 years hence, represents the author's projection of the scientific knowledge of today. Scientific progress is moving at an accelerating pace, and if that pace is maintained, it seems fair to assume that the conception herein described will, 750 years hence, be found to have fallen far short of the actual progress made in the interim.

HUGO GERNSBACK

September 3, 1925

FOREWORD

BY LEE DE FOREST, Ph.D., D.Sc., D.Eng.
Father of Radio

No BOOK in two generations, no book since Jules Verne, has undertaken to do what Hugo Gernsback in the first decade of our century has here so outstandingly achieved.

He is gifted with a mind eternally alert, trained from childhood to observe and think. His unbridled imagination has ever fed on the facts of science and technology which his habit of omniverous reading has been continually storing within his brain. As result of this unusual combination his tireless energies have been directed, since childhood in Luxembourg, to writing popular science in a fashion peculiarly attractive to young men and boys who, like himself, possess a keen interest in all realms of physical Nature.

His first essay in this field was his monthly magazine, *Modern Electrics*, the first to attempt to outline in language understandable by American youth the newly developing science of *wireless communication*. He made of this first venture into the publishing business a medium wherein, amid serious newsy articles regarding current electrical developments, his eager imagination could find full play. The most outstanding, most extraordinary prophecies which this young clairvoyant had at that time conceived—all based on his keen observations and appreciation of their real significance and trend—he chose to record in the guise of a fanciful romance bearing the strange, cabalistic title of this book.

The author, even at that early date (1911) had a clear conception of future television, then quite unheard of, almost undreamed of. He dubs it "Telephot" and outlines its revolutionary utilities. His hero, Ralph, explains to his enamorata how man has mastered weather-control. Only today has a professor shown New York City how to end its water famine by man-made torrential rains. Years in advance of their advent he describes libraries of micro-film projected on large screens; and news printed electrolytically, without printer's ink. Today we begin to read of this as being partially commercialized. His "Menograph," or thought recorder, is today crudely realized in our lie-detector. By means of his "Hypnobioscope" most of scholastic studying is done while the pupil sleeps. Who is bold enough to scoff at the possibility of such a delightful method? For one, not I.

"Most of the studying was done while one slept," explains Ralph—a statement truly applicable to many a somnolent student's performance today!

Ralph explains, as of the year 2660, the resuscitation of animal (human) life years after the body has been drained of blood. Yet only yesterday a Russian doctor claims to have accomplished this "miracle." His 750-year future has already begun to be realized. Many Utopias are here foretold, such as absolutely permanent non-wearing, metallic highways, where trolley-cars and gas-driven autos are only ancient memories, long obsolete.

"Only electrobiles were to be seen." Here the author badly misjudged the future trend of auto-travel, *away* from the electric.

He foresaw far better night-illuminated streets than we have yet attained. Let us hope that we must not wait 750 years until cities are "as bright by night as by day"; nor New York's climate, man-controlled, to be "the finest on Earth," with temperatures perennially at 72, sunshine all day, rain for one hour only, every night! In that future we shall have reliable transfer of sun energy into electric by means of photo-electric elements responsive to ultra-violet radiation.

In Musak we already have the wide distribution of music which Mr. Gernsback foresaw in 1911; also our night baseball games, then first foretold. His airplanes launching from roof-tops we partly realize already in our helicopter mail service. But instead of his agglomeration of colored light-beams for direction of aviation we have the far reaching radio beacons, coupled with Loran.

Even today's mysterious "flying saucers" he foretold with nice detail!

Foreseeing the vast increase in global population (the world's gravest menace) Ralph has so deftly applied science to plant growth that we shall reap four crops of wheat per year in sun-heated glass houses of county-sized acreage, to feed the new billions. He fears not an overcrowded, 200 million metropolitan New York!

Only today I read of a recent system for using heat from deep earth for house-warming, now being commercialized. "Ralph" described the same arrangement forty years ago!

Here is liquid fertilizer sprayed as a crop accelerator; and plant-root stimulation by means of high-frequency currents, wholesale diathermy applied to farming; and many other improvements in farm procedure which make this book profitable reading for today's science-minded farmers.

The author foresaw a much-to-be-desired manufacture of news-print from the resultant excessive growth of grain stocks, thereby terminating today's wanton destruction of our forests for comic supplements and sexy pulps.

Last year in the Bell Laboratories I witnessed the recording on paper of the complexities of my voice, very much as Ralph described it in 1911 to his A.D. 2660 friends.

As to the plausibility of Ralph's conquest of gravitation I refer the reader to the recently published General Field Equations of Dr. Einstein. Ralph insisted, even in 1911, that gravitation is indeed wave form, similar to the electromagnetic, and that by interference there—between the force of gravitation may be partially nullified. Let us wait until 2660 to see if he was correctly reported. This and many other strange things our descendants *may* see.

But to me the most impressive pages of this strange book are those that outlined with striking clarity the basic idea of radar as we know it today. Although gummed over with reference to imaginary metals, interplanetary ships travelling at comet speeds, and a very earthy romance, the uncanny foresight of Hugo Gernsback in 1911 into the realities of World War II constitutes perhaps the most amazing paragraphs in this astonishing Book of Prophecy.

Chicago, Ill.
May 1950

FOREWORD

BY FLETCHER PRATT

THIS IS a book of historic importance, which belongs on the shelves of a variety of types of people, though not for the usual reasons why a fictional work is a must. No one will ever compare *Ralph 124C 41 +* with the novels of Marcel Proust or even those of Robert Louis Stevenson. The story is the simplest kind of romantic adventure tale and characters are not particularly significant as such. What matters is the view from the windows as the train runs through the landscape.

For it is a book of prophecy, one of the most remarkable ever written. It has long since been a gold mine for nearly every writer of science-fiction during a generation. No author laying his story in the future would think today of doing without Mr. Gernsback's three-dimensional color television, and very few without his satellite city circling the Earth; and no reader would think of questioning the feasibility of these devices.

The very method employed in the book, that of supplying the people of the future with technical inventions which are the logical outgrowths of those currently in use or logically developed from currently accepted principles—this method has become fundamental in science-fiction. Indeed, it may be said to constitute that new art; and in a very proper sense, *Ralph 124C 41 +* may be called the first science-fiction story ever written.

This will doubtless bring some protest from the admirers of Mr. H. G. Wells. But a little thought will show that, in spite of some arresting and rather wonderful pictures of the future, and some extremely ingenious scientific devices described, Mr. Wells was not really writing science-fiction. There is nothing known to science out of which the time machine could be developed; Wells simply tells us that it was built and goes on with his story. The invincible balloon-battleships in *The War in the Air* are flatly contradictory to logic; even when the book was written, everybody knew that hydrogen is inflammable. Heat dissipates in air far too rapidly to allow the heat-ray camera of the Martians in *The War of the Worlds* to be built; and a very brief consideration will show that the construction of the anti-gravity plates in *The First Men in the Moon* would be child's play beside the problem of constructing the screens which temporarily kept those plates from working.

It is the same all down the line, and with Jules Verne as well—whose passengers in the moon-shell would be killed at the moment of firing. The fact is that Wells, himself enough of a scientist to use technical terms correctly, was afflicted with low scientific morality where fiction was concerned. He tried to be a prophet in the domain of sociology, but he was not really interested in the progress of physical science. As long as he could get his characters into a situation by means of a plausible-sounding device, he was quite willing to flim-flam the reader about the practicability of the device and the soundness of the principles involved.

Mr. Gernsback, on the other hand, founded the school

of fiction in which the technical plausibility of the sur-
roundings is at least as important as the literary plausibility of the characters. For that matter, the reader is besought
to show some interest in what can be done for us by the
chemist, the inventor, the electrician, and even the meteor-
ologist. It has often been pointed out that these technicians
cannot change human nature, but Mr. Gernsback indicates
that they can put human nature into a position where it
can hardly avoid changing itself. World government is not
an impossibility in an atmosphere where any person on the
planet can be instantly in visible communication with any
other, and where the barrier of language can be thrown
down during a night's sleep.

Thanks to the rules he set for himself (and also, no
doubt, to his wide acquaintance with that region in which
all the sciences are applied to the practical service of man
in the form of inventions) Mr. Gernsback has been rather
astoundingly successful in predicting actual developments.
Ralph 124C 41 + was written in 1911. The writer's most
famous hit, of course, is *radar* (p. 152), which no one
else had come near to conceiving at the time. Yet his description will do as a fair working description of radar as
it is today. The device here called "the hypnobioscope"
(p. 49) for teaching during sleep, has not been developed to the extent described in the story, but works in a
limited fashion and is obviously capable of extension. On
p. 116 artificial silk and wool are produced by a process so
much like that currently used in the manufacture of rayon
and nylon that one wonders whether Mr. Gernsback has
a share in the patents. Rustproof alloy steel (p. 103),
magnesium alloys in light-weight construction (p. 29),
televised opera performances (p. 86), vending machines

(p. 89), packing in paper-thin sheets of metal (p. 89)—are all things we know about today but which only Hugo Gernsback could have conceived in 1911.

In addition, there are a number of items where the essential correctness of the concept may be concealed from the reader by the terms employed in this book—for it is not granted to prophets to foresee what words will be employed when inventors designate their products. The "glass" furniture (p. 25) has been made good in the form of plastics—which are, technically, glasses. Fluorescent lighting appears on p. 30 under the name of "luminor." The electric elevator (p. 43) has not turned up as an elevator, but its mechanism is used to drive the electric torpedoes which sank much of the Japanese merchant marine during the war. Newspapers are printed on microfilm on p. 46, and the trans-Uranium elements show up on p. 53. Baseball and football are played at night on p. 80 and paper is made from straw on p. 104. A device which is essentially the radio-direction-finder is on p. 120, and on p. 128 there is a recording mechanism which differs from today's wire-recorders only in employing a strip of paper scanned by light, and which has since been built. This by no means exhausts the list, but it would detract from the reader's enjoyment not to allow him to make some discoveries for himself.

To be sure, there are certain inaccuracies. The under-earth tube from France to New York does not seem a good engineering proposition today. Nobody understood the nature of radium emanation in 1911 and neither did Mr. Gernsback. But the percentage of accurate judgments (one cannot call them guesses, when they are so numerous and so close to the mark) is somewhere up in the nineties.

Which leads one to the thought that this book perhaps has an importance beyond that as a literary and historical curiosity. Not all the predictions have been fulfilled or placed beyond fulfillment; and if research had proceeded along the lines of (for instance) Mr. Gernsback's suggestion for radar, we might have had that device a good deal earlier. In *Ralph 124C 41 +* the weather is under complete control. We seem to be edging in that direction, but maybe a little more push is needed—the kind of push that could be supplied by a book like this. Medical research has now caught up with Gernsback by deciding that thought in the human brain is accompanied by electrical manifestations; on p. 48 this concept has advanced to the point where thoughts can be recorded on a tape in the form of interpretable graphs, and it may become true in practice if someone works on the problem. The idea of draining off all the blood from a living body for purification and then replacing it (transfusion also ranks as a Gernsback prediction) is today far from fantastic. It is the standard and only treatment for RH newborn infants.

Yet perhaps the most interesting of all the predictions is that regarding space flight. (Incidentally, the physical and psychological effects of space travel are worked out with a care that would be worth the attention of some current science-fiction writers.) In the days of *Ralph 124C 41 +*, this is not accomplished by means of the rockets everyone is talking about at present, but by using a gravity neutralizer.

But be it noticed that this is not the mysterious metal of H. G. Wells. Gernsback does it in a technically explicable and plausible way, by means of a metal grid, electrically (or electronically) excited. Today it is as possible to do this as it was to build a radar set in 1911; that is, not at all. But the new formula of Dr. Einstein, at last integrating gravity with other manifestations, makes it seem probable that it is not beyond hope to screen gravitation from a selected area; and when that happens, Mr. Gernsback's educated imagination, which has preceded the normal human mind to so many things on Earth, will have led the way to the stars.

New York, May 1950

1

THE AVALANCHE

As THE *vibrations* died down in the laboratory the big man arose from the glass chair and viewed the complicated apparatus on the table. It was complete to the last detail. He glanced at the calendar. It was September 1st in the year 2660. Tomorrow was to be a big and busy day for him, for it was to witness the final phase of the three-year experiment. He yawned and stretched himself to his full height, revealing a physique much larger than that of the average man of his times and approaching that of the huge Martians.

His physical superiority, however, was as nothing compared to his gigantic mind. He was *Ralph 124C 41 +*, one of the greatest living scientists and *one of the ten men on the whole planet earth permitted to use the Plus sign after his name.* Stepping to the *Telephot* on the side of the wall he pressed a group of buttons and in a few minutes the faceplate of the Telephot became luminous, revealing the face of a clean shaven man about thirty, a pleasant but serious face.

As soon as he recognized the face of Ralph in his own Telephot he smiled and said, "Hello Ralph."

"Hello Edward, I wanted to ask you if you could come over to the laboratory tomorrow morning. I have something unusually interesting to show you. Look!"

He stepped to one side of his instrument so that his friend could see the apparatus on the table about ten feet from the Telephot faceplate.

Edward came closer to his own faceplate, in order that he might see further into the laboratory.

"Why, you've finished it!" he exclaimed. "And your famous—"

At this moment the voice ceased and Ralph's faceplate became clear. Somewhere in the Teleservice company's central office the connection had been broken. After several vain efforts to restore it Ralph was about to give up in disgust and leave the Telephot when the instrument began to glow again. But instead of the face of his friend there appeared that of a vivacious beautiful girl. She was in evening dress and behind her on a table stood a lighted lamp.

Startled at the face of an utter stranger, an unconscious Oh! escaped her lips, to which Ralph quickly replied:

"I beg your pardon, but 'Central' seems to have made another mistake. I shall certainly have to make a complaint about the service."

Her reply indicated that the mistake of "Central" was a little out of the ordinary, for he had been swung onto the Intercontinental Service as he at once understood when she said, *"Pardon, Monsieur, je ne comprends pas!"*

He immediately turned the small shining disc of the Language Rectifier on his instrument till the pointer rested on *"French."*

"The service mistakes are very annoying," he heard her say in perfect English. Realizing however, that she was hardly being courteous to the pleasant looking young man who was smiling at her she added, "But sometimes Central's 'mistakes' may be forgiven, depending, of course, on the patience and courtesy of the other person involved."

This, Ralph appreciated, was an attempt at mollification with perhaps a touch of coquetry.

Nevertheless he bowed in acknowledgment of the pretty speech.

She was now closer to the faceplate and was looking with curious eyes at the details of the laboratory—one of the finest in the world.

"What a strange place! What is it, and where are you?" she asked naïvely.

"New York," he drawled.

"That's a long way from here," she said brightly. "I wonder if you know where I am?"

"I can make a pretty shrewd guess," he returned. "To begin with, before I rectified your speech you spoke French, hence you are probably French. Secondly, you have a lamp burning in your room although it is only four o'clock in the afternoon here in New York. You also wear evening dress. It must be evening, and inasmuch as the clock on your mantelpiece points to nine I would say you are in France, as New York time is five hours ahead of French time."

"Clever, but not quite right. I am not French nor do I live in France. I am Swiss and I live in western Switzerland. Swiss time, you know, is almost the same as French time."

Both laughed. Suddenly she said:

"Your face looks so familiar to me, it seems I must have seen you before."

"That is possible," he admitted somewhat embarrassed. "You have perhaps seen one of my pictures."

"How stupid of me!" she exclaimed. "Why of course I should have recognized you immediately. You are the great American inventor, Ralph 124C 41 +."

He again smiled and she continued:

"How interesting your work must be and just think how *perfectly* lovely that I should be so fortunate as to make your acquaintance in this manner. Fancy, the great Ralph 124C 41 + who always denies himself to society."

She hesitated, and then, impulsively, "I wonder if it would be too much to ask you for your autograph?"

Much to his astonishment Ralph found himself pleased with the request. Autograph-hunting women he usually dismissed with a curt refusal.

"Certainly," he answered, "but it seems only fair that I should know to whom I am giving it."

"Oh," she said, blushing a little, and then, with dancing eyes, "Why?"

"Because," replied Ralph with an audacity that surprised himself, "I don't want to be put to the necessity of calling up all Switzerland to find you again."

"Well, if you put it that way," she said, the scarlet mounting in her cheeks, "I suppose I must. *I am Alice* 212B 423, of Ventalp, Switzerland."

Ralph then attached the Telautograph to his Telephot while the girl did the same. When both instruments were connected he signed his name and he saw his signature appear simultaneously on the machine in Switzerland.

"Thank you so much!" she exclaimed, and added, "I am really proud to have your autograph. From what I have heard of you this is the first you have ever given to a lady. Am I right?" she asked.

"You are perfectly correct, and what is more, it affords

me a very great pleasure indeed to present it to you."

"How lovely," she said as she held up the autograph, "I have never seen an original signature with the +, for there are only ten of you who have it on this planet, and now to actually *have* one seems almost unbelievable."

The awe and admiration in her dark eyes began to make him feel a little uncomfortable. She sensed this immediately and once more became apologetic.

"I shouldn't take up your time in this manner," she went on, "but you see, I have not spoken to any living being for five days and I am just dying to talk."

"Go right ahead, I am delighted to listen. What caused your isolation?"

"Well, you see," she answered, "father and I live in our villa half way up Mount Rosa, and for the last five days such a terrible blizzard has been raging that the house is entirely snowed in. The storm was so terrific that no aero-flyer could come near the house; I have never seen such a thing. Five days ago my father and brother left for Paris, intending to return the same afternoon, but they had a bad accident in which my brother dislocated his knee-cap; both were, therefore, obliged to stay somewhere near Paris, where they landed, and in the meanwhile the blizzard set in. The Teleservice line became disconnected somewhere in the valley, and this is the first connection I have had for five days. How they came to connect me with New York, though, is a puzzle!"

"Most extraordinary—but how about the Radio?"

"Both the Power mast and the Communico mast were blown down the same day, and I was left without any means of communication whatever. However, I managed to put the light magnesium power mast into a temporary position again, and I had just called up the Teleservice Company, telling them again to direct the power, and getting some other information when they cut me in on you."

"Yes, I knew something was wrong when I saw the old-fashioned Radialamp in your room, and I could not quite understand it. You had better try the power now; they probably have directed it by this time; anyhow, the Luminor should work."

"You are probably right," and raising her voice, she called out sharply: *"Lux!"*

The delicate detectophone mechanism of the Luminor responded instantly to her command; and the room was flooded at once with the beautiful cold pink-white Luminor-light, emanating from the thin wire running around the four sides of the room below the white ceiling.

The light, however, seemed too strong, and she sharply cried, *"Lux-dah!"* The mechanism again responded; the cold light-radiation of the Luminor wire decreased in intensity at once and the room appeared in an exquisite pink light.

"That's better now," she laughed. "The heater just begins to get warm, too. I am frozen stiff; just think, no heat for five days! I really sometimes envy our ancestors, who, I believe, heated their houses with stoves, burning strange black rocks or tree-chunks in them!"

"That's too bad! It must be a dreadful predicament to be cut off from the entire world, in these days of weather control. It must be a novel experience. I cannot understand, however, what should have brought on a blizzard in midsummer."

"Unfortunately, our governor had some trouble with

the four weather-engineers of our district, some months ago, and they struck for better living. They claimed the authorities did not furnish them with sufficient luxuries, and when their demands were refused, they simultaneously turned on the high-depression at the four Meteoro-Towers and then fled, leaving their towers with the high-tension currents escaping at a tremendous rate.

"This was done in the evening, and by midnight our entire district, bounded by the four Meteoro-Towers, was covered with two inches of snow. They had erected especially, additional discharge arms, pointing downward from the towers, for the purpose of snowing in the Meteoros completely.

"Their plans were well laid, for it became impossible to approach the towers for four days; and they finally had to be dismantled by directed energy from forty other Meteoro-Towers, which directed a tremendous amount of energy against the four local towers, till the latter were fused and melted.

"The other Meteoros, I believe, will start in immediately to direct a low-pression over our district; but, as they are not very near us, it will probably take them twenty-four hours to generate enough heat to melt the snow and ice. They will probably encounter considerable difficulty, because our snowed-under district naturally will give rise to some meteorological disturbances in their own districts, and therefore they will be obliged, I presume, to take care of the weather conditions in their districts as well as our own."

"What a remarkable case!" Ralph ejaculated.

She opened her mouth as if to say something. But at that moment an electric gong began to ring furiously, so loud that it vibrated loudly in Ralph's laboratory, four thousand miles away.

Immediately her countenance changed, and the smile in her eyes gave way to a look of terror.

"What is that?" Ralph asked sharply.

"An avalanche! It's just started—what shall I do, oh, what shall I do! It'll reach here in fifteen minutes and I'm absolutely helpless. Tell me—what shall I do?"

The mind of the scientist reacted instantly.

"Speak quick!" he barked. "Is your Power Mast still up?"

"Yes, but what good—?"

"Never mind. Your wave length?"

".629."

"Oscillatory?"

"491,211."

"Can you direct it yourself?"

"Yes."

"Could you attach a six-foot piece of your blown-down Communico mast to the base of the Power aerial?"

"Certainly—it's of alomagnesium and it is very light."

"Good! Now act quick! Run to the roof and attach the Communico mastpiece to the very base of the power mast, and point the former towards the avalanche. Then move the directoscope exactly to West-by-South, and point the antenna of the power mast East-by-North. Now run—I'll do the rest!"

He saw her drop the receiver and rush away from the Telephot. Immediately he leaped up the glass stairs to the top of his building, and swung his big aerial around so that it pointed West-by-South.

He then adjusted his directoscope till a little bell began to ring. He knew then that the instrument was in perfect tune with the far-off instrument in Switzerland; he also noted that its pointer had swung to exactly East-by-North.

"So far, so good," he whistled with satisfaction. "Now for the power!"

He ran down to the laboratory and threw in a switch. Then he threw in another one with his foot, while clasping his ears tightly with his rubber-gloved hands. A terrible, whining sound was heard, and the building shook. It was the warning siren on top of the house, which could be heard within a radius of sixty miles, sounding its warning to all to keep away from tall steel or metal structures, or, if they could not do this, to insulate themselves.

He sounded the siren twice for ten seconds, which meant that he would direct his ultra-power for at least twenty minutes, and everybody must be on guard for this length of time.

No sooner had the siren blast stopped, than he had seen Alice at the Telephot, signalling him that everything was in readiness.

He yelled to her to insulate herself, and he saw her jump into a tall glass chair where she sat perfectly still, deathly white. He could see that she clasped her hands to her ears; and he knew that she must be trying to shut out the thunder of the descending avalanche.

He ran up his high glass ladder; and having reached the top, began to turn the large glass wheel the shaft of which was connected with the ultra-generator.

As he started turning the wheel, for the first time he

33

looked at the clock. He observed that it was just nine minutes after he first had heard the gong and he smiled, coldly. He knew he was in time.

A terrifying roar set in as soon as he had commenced to turn the wheel. It was as if a million devils had been let loose. Sparks were flying everywhere. Small metal parts not encased in lead boxes fused. Long streamers of blue flames emanated from sharp objects, while ball-shaped objects glowed with a white aureole.

Large iron pieces became strongly magnetic, and small iron objects continually flew from one large iron piece to another. Ralph's watch chain became so hot that he had to discard it, together with his watch.

He kept on turning the wheel, and the roar changed to a scream so intense that he had to pull out his rubber ear vacuum-caps so that he might not hear the terrible sound. As he turned the wheel farther around the tone of the ultra-generator reached the note where it coincided with the fundamental note of the building, which was built of steelonium (the new substitute for steel).

Suddenly the whole building "sang," with a shriek so loud and piercing that it could be heard twenty miles away.

Another building whose fundamental note was the same began to "sing" in its turn, just as one tuning fork produces sympathetic sounds in a similar distant one.

A few more turns of the wheel and the "singing" stopped. As he continued turning the wheel of the generator, the latter gave out sounds sharper and sharper, higher and higher, shriller and shriller, till the shrieking became unendurable.

And then, suddenly, all sound stopped abruptly.

The frequency had passed over twenty thousand, at which point the human ear ceases to hear sounds.

Ralph turned the wheel a few more notches and then stopped. Except for the flying iron pieces, there was no sound. Even the myriads of sparks leaping around were strangely silent, except for the hissing noise of flames streaming from sharp metal points.

Ralph looked at the clock. It was exactly ten minutes after the first sounding of the gong. He then turned the wheel one notch further and instantly the room was plunged into pitch-black darkness.

To anyone unacquainted with the tremendous force under the control of Ralph 124C 41 +, but having the temerity to insulate himself and stand on a nearby roof there would have been visible an unusual sight. He would also have undergone some remarkable experiences.

The uninitiated stranger standing—well insulated—on a roof not very far off from Ralph's laboratory, would have witnessed the following remarkable phenomena:

As soon as Ralph threw the power of the Ultra-Generator on his aerial, the latter began to shoot out hissing flames in the direction of West-by-South.

As Ralph kept turning on more power, the flames became longer and the sound louder. The heavy iridium wires of the large aerial became red-hot, then yellow, then dazzling white, and the entire mast became white-hot. Just as the observer could hardly endure the shrill hissing sound of the outflowing flames any more, the sound stopped altogether, abruptly, and simultaneously the whole landscape was plunged into such a pitch-black darkness as he had never experienced before. He could not even see his hand before his eyes. The aerial could not be seen either, although he could feel the tremendous energy still flowing away.

What had happened? The aerial on top of Ralph's house had obtained such a tremendously high frequency, and had become so strongly energyzed, that it acted toward the ether much the same as a vacuum pump acts on the air.

The aerial for a radius of some forty miles attracted the ether so fast that a new supply could not spread over this area with sufficient rapidity.

Inasmuch as light waves cannot pass through space without the medium of ether, *it necessarily follows that the entire area upon which the aerial acted was dark.*

The observer who had never before been in an etherless hole (the so-called negative whirlpool), experienced some remarkable sensations during the twenty minutes that followed.

It is a well known fact that heat waves cannot pass through space without their medium, ether, the same as an electric bell, working in a vacuum, cannot be heard outside of the vacuum, because sound waves cannot pass through space without their medium, the air.

No sooner had the darkness set in, than a peculiar feeling of numbness and passiveness would have come over him.

As long as he was in the etherless space, *he absolutely stopped growing older,* as no combustion nor digestion can go on without ether. *He furthermore had lost all sense of heat or cold.* His pipe, hot previously, was neither hot nor cold to his touch. His own body could not grow cold as its heat could not be given off to the atmosphere, nor could his body grow cold, even if he had sat on a cake of ice, because there was no ether to permit the heat to pass from one atom to another.

He would have remembered how, one day, he had been in a tornado center, and how, when the storm center had created a partial vacuum around him, he all of a sudden had felt the very air drawn from his lungs. He would have remembered people talking about an air-less hole, in which there was no medium but ether (inasmuch as he could see the light). Now things were reversed. He could hear and breathe, because the ether has no effect on these functions; but he had been robbed of his visual senses, and heat or cold could not affect him, as there was no means by which the heat or cold could traverse the ether-hole.

Alice's father, who had heard of the strike of the Meteoro-Tower operators and guessed of his daughter's predicament, rushed back from Paris in his aeroflyer. He had speeded up his machine to the utmost, scenting impending disaster as if by instinct. When finally his villa came into sight, his blood froze in his veins and his heart stopped beating at the scene below him.

He could see that an immense avalanche was sweeping down the mountain-side, with his house, that sheltered his daughter, directly in the path of it.

As he approached, he heard the roar and thunder of the avalanche as it swept everything in its path before it. He knew he was powerless, as he could not reach the house in time, and it only meant the certain destruction of himself if he could; and for that reason he could do nothing but be a spectator of the tragedy which would enact itself before his eyes in a few short minutes.

At this juncture a miracle, so it seemed to the distracted father, occurred.

His eye chanced to fall on the Power mast on the top of his house. He could see the iridium aerial wires which were pointing East-by-North suddenly become red-hot; then yellow, then white-hot, at the same time he felt that some enormous etheric disturbance had been set up, as sparks were flying from all metallic parts of his machine. When he looked again at the aerial on his house, he saw that a piece of the Communico mast, which apparently had fallen at the base of the Power mast, and which was pointing directly at the avalanche, was streaming gigantic flames which grew longer and longer, and gave forth shriller and shriller sounds. The flames which streamed from the end of the Communico-mast-piece looked like a tremendously long jet of water leaving its nozzle under pressure.

For about five hundred yards from the tip of the Communico mast it was really only a single flame about fifteen feet in diameter. Beyond that it spread out fan-wise. He could also see that the entire Power mast, including the Communico mast, was glowing in a white heat, showing that immense forces were directed upon it. By this time the avalanche had almost come in contact with the furthest end of the flames.

Here the unbelievable happened. No sooner did the avalanche touch the flames, than it began turning to water. It seemed that the heat of those flames was so intense and powerful that had the avalanche been a block of solid ice it would not have made any marked difference. As it was, the entire avalanche was being reduced to hot water and steam even before it reached the main shaft of the flame.

A torrent of hot water rushing down the mountain was all that remained of the menacing avalanche; and while the water did some damage, it was insignificant.

For several minutes after the melting of the avalanche the flames continued to stream from the aerial, and then faded away.

Ralph 124C 41 +, in New York, four thousand miles distant, had turned off the power of his ultra-generator.

He climbed down his glass ladder, stepped over to the Telephot, and found that Alice had already reached her instrument.

She looked at the man smiling in the faceplate of the Telephot almost dumb with an emotion that came very near to being reverence.

The voice that reached him was trembling and he could see her struggle for coherent speech.

"It's gone," she gasped; "what *did* you do?"

"Melted it."

"Melted it!" she echoed, "I—"

Before she could continue, the door in her room burst violently open and in rushed a fear-stricken old man. Alice flew to his arms, crying, "Oh father—"

Ralph 124C 41 + with discretion disconnected the Telephot.

2

TWO FACES

FEELING THE NEED of fresh air and quiet after the strain of the last half hour, Ralph 124C 41 + climbed the few steps leading from the laboratory to the roof and sat down on a bench beneath the revolving aerial.

The hum of the great city came faintly from below. Aeroflyers dotted the sky. From time to time, trans-oceanic or trans-continental air liners passed with a low vibration, scarcely audible.

At times a great air-craft would come close—within 500 yards perhaps—when the passengers would crane their necks to get a good view of his "house," if such it could be called.

Indeed, his "house," which was a round tower, 650 feet high, and thirty in diameter, built entirely of crystal glass-bricks and steelonium, was one of the sights of New York. A grateful city, recognizing his genius and his benefits to humanity, had erected the great tower for him on a plot where, centuries ago, Union Square had been.

The top of the tower was twice as great in circumference as the main building, and in this upper part was located the research laboratory, famous throughout the world. An electro-magnetic tube elevator ran down the tower on one side of the building, all the rooms being circular in shape, except for the space taken up by the elevator.

Ralph, sitting on the roof of his tower, was oblivious to all about him. He was unable to dismiss from his mind the lovely face of the girl whose life he had just been the means of saving. The soft tones of her voice were in his ears. Heretofore engrossed in his work, his scientific mind had been oblivious to women. They had played no part in his life. Science had been his mistress, and a laboratory his home.

And now, in one short half hour, for him the whole world had become a new place. Two dark eyes, a bewitching pair of lips, a voice that had stirred the very core of his being—

Ralph shook himself. It was not for him to think of these things, he told himself. He was but a tool, a tool to advance science, to benefit humanity. He belonged, not to himself, but to the Government—the Government, who fed and clothed him, and whose doctors guarded his health with every precaution. He had to pay the penalty of his +. To be sure, he had everything. He had but to ask and his wish was law—if it did not interfere with his work.

There were times he grew restive under the restraint, he longed to smoke the tobacco forbidden him by watchful doctors, and to indulge in those little vices which vary the monotony of existence for the ordinary individual. There were times when he most ardently wished that he *were* an ordinary individual.

He was not allowed to make dangerous tests personally, thereby endangering a life invaluable to the Government. That institution would supply him with some criminal under sentence of death who would be compelled to undergo the test for him. If the criminal were killed during the experiment, nothing was lost; if he did not perish, he would be imprisoned for life.

Being a true scientist, Ralph wanted to make his own dangerous experiments. Not to do this took away the very spice of life for him, and on occasion he rebelled. He would call up the Planet Governor, the ruler of 15 billion human beings, and demand that he be relieved of his work.

"I can't stand it," he would protest. "This constraint which I am forced to endure maddens me, I feel that I am being hampered."

The Governor, a wise man, and a kindly one, would often call upon him in person, and for a long time they would discuss the question, Ralph protesting, the Governor reasoning with him.

"I am nothing but a prisoner," Ralph stormed once.

"You are a great inventor," smiled the Governor, "and a tremendous factor in the world's advancement. You are invaluable to humanity, and—you are irreplaceable. You belong to the world—not to yourself."

Many times in the past few years he recalled, had the two been over the same ground, and many times had the diplomatic Governor convinced the scientist that in sacrifice of self and devotion to the world's future lay his great reward.

The voice of his manservant interrupted his reverie.

"Sir," he said, "your presence in the transmission-room would be appreciated."

"What is it?" asked the scientist, impatient at the interruption.

"Sir, the people have heard all about the Switzerland incident of an hour ago and desire to show their appreciation."

"Well, I suppose I must submit," the inventor rather wearily responded, and both stepped over into the round steel car of the electromagnetic elevator. The butler pressed one of the 28 ivory buttons and the car shot downward, with neither noise nor friction. There were no cables or guides, the car being held and propelled by magnetism only. At the 22nd floor the car stopped, and Ralph stepped into the transmission-room.

No sooner had he entered than the deafening applause of hundreds of thousands of voices greeted him, and he was forced to put his hands to his ears to muffle the sound.

Yet, the transmission-room was entirely empty.

Every inch of the wall, however, was covered with large-sized Telephots and loud-speaking devices.

Centuries ago, when people tendered some one an ovation, they would all assemble in some great square or large hall. The celebrity would have to appear in person, else there would be no ovation—truly a clumsy means. Then, too, in those years, people at a distance could neither see nor hear what was going on throughout the world.

Ralph's ovation was the result of the enterprise of a news "paper" which had issued extras about his exploit, and urged its readers to be connected with him at 5 p. m.

Naturally everyone who could spare the time had called the Teleservice Company and asked to be connected with the inventor's trunk-line—and this was the result.

Ralph 124C 41 + stepped into the middle of the room

43

and bowed to the four points of the compass, in order that all might see him perfectly. The noise was deafening, and as it rather grew in volume than diminished he beseechingly held up his hands. In a few seconds the applause ceased and some one cried—"Speech!"

Ralph spoke briefly, thanking his audience for their interest, and touching but lightly upon his rescue of the young Swiss girl, begged his hearers to remember that in no way had he risked his life and therefore could scarcely be called a hero.

Vociferous cries of "No, no," told him that no one shared his humble opinion of the achievement.

It was at this juncture that Ralph's attention was caught by two persons in the audience. There were so many thousands of faces on each plate that nearly every countenance was blurred, due to their constant movement. (He himself, however, was clearly seen by them, as each one had switched on their "reversers," making it possible to see only the object at the end of the line.)

To Ralph, the shifting, clouded appearance of his audience was a commonplace.

This was not the first time that he had been called upon to receive the thanks of the multitude for some unusual service he had rendered them, or some surprising scientific feat he had successfully accomplished. While realizing that he must of necessity yield to public adulation, it more or less bored him.

He was not particularly interested in the crowd, either collectively or individually, and as there were so many faces crowded into each faceplate he made no attempt to distinguish friends from strangers.

Yet there were two faces among the numerous Telephot faceplates that Ralph in making his brief speech, found his eyes returning to again and again. Each occupied the whole of a respective faceplate and while dissimilar in appearance, nevertheless were markedly alike in expression. It was as if they were studying this great scientist, endeavoring to fix in their minds a permanent picture of him. Ralph sensed no animosity in their steady almost hypnotic gaze and yet they were curiously apart from the enthusiastic throng. He felt as though he were, to both of them, under the microscope.

One of the faces was that of a man in his early thirties. It was a handsome face, though, to the close observer, the eyes were set just a trifle too near together, and the mouth betrayed cunning and had a touch of viciousness.

The other was not a Terrestrial, but a visiting Martian. It was impossible to mistake the distinctly Martian cast of countenance. The great black horse eyes in the long, melancholy face, the elongated slightly pointed ears were proof enough. Martians in New York were not sufficiently rare to excite any particular comment. Many made that city their permanent home, although the law on the planet Earth, as well as on Mars, which forbade the intermarriage of Martians and Terrestrials, kept them from flocking earthwards in any great numbers.

In the applause that followed the conclusion of Ralph's words the incident of the two pairs of scrutinizing eyes vanished from his thoughts. But his subconscious self, that marvelous mechanism which forgets nothing, had photographed them indelibly. With the plaudits of the crowd still ringing he bowed and left the room.

He went, via the elevator, directly to his library, and asked for the afternoon news.

His man handed him a tray on which lay a piece of material *as large as a postage stamp,* as transparent and flexible as celluloid.

"What edition is this?" he asked.

"The 5 o'clock *New York News,*[*] sir."

Ralph took the "News" and placed it in a metal holder which was part of the hinged door of a small box. He closed the door and turned on a switch on the side of the box. Immediately there appeared on the opposite white wall of the room, a twelve-column page of the *New York News* and the scientist, leaning back in his chair, proceeded to read.

The *New York News* was simply a microscopic reduction of a page, which, when enlarged by a powerful lens, became plainly visible.

Moreover, each paper had eight "pages," in separate sheets, as was the fashion centuries ago, but eight pages literally on top of each other. The printing process was electrolytic, no ink whatsoever being used in the manufacture of the "newspaper." This process was invented in 1910 by an Englishman, and improved by the American 64L 52 in 2031, who made it possible to "print" *in one operation* eight different subjects, *one on top of another.*

These eight impressions could be made visible only by subjecting the "paper" to different colors, the color rays bringing out the different prints. The seven colors of the rainbow were used, while white light was employed to show reproduced photographs, etc., in their natural colors. With this method it was possible to "print" a "newspaper," fully ten times as large in volume as any newspaper

[*] At the time this was written there was no newspaper of that name.

of the 21st century, on a piece of film, the size of a postage-stamp.

Each paper published an edition every 30 minutes, and if one did not possess a projector, one could read the "paper" by inserting the *News* in a holder beneath a powerful lens which one carried in one's pocket, folded when not in use. To read the eight different pages, a revolving color screen was placed directly underneath the lens, to bring out the different colors necessary to read the "paper."

Ralph, 124C 41 +, glancing over the head-lines of his *News,* saw that considerable space was given to his latest exploit, the paper showing actual photographs of the Swiss Alpine scene, which a correspondent had taken as the avalanche thundered down the mountain. The photographs had been sent by *Teleradiograph* immediately after the occurrence in Switzerland, and the *News* had printed them in all the *natural* colors twenty minutes after Ralph had turned off the ultra-power in New York.

These photographs seemed to be the only thing that interested Ralph, as they showed the house and the surrounding Alps. These, with the monstrous avalanche in progression photographed and reproduced in the natural colors, were very impressive.

Presently he revolved the color screen of his projector to green—the technical page of the *News*—to him the most interesting reading in the paper.

He soon had read all that interested him, and as there was still an hour before dinner time he began to "write" his lecture: "On the prolongation of animal life by π-Rays."

He attached a double leather head-band to his head.

At each end of the band was attached a round metal disc that pressed closely on the temples. From each metal disc an insulated wire led to a small square box, the *Menograph,* or mind-writer.

He then pressed a button and a low humming was heard; simultaneously two small bulbs began to glow with a soft green fluorescent light. Grasping a button connected with a flexible cord to the Menograph, he leaned back in his chair.

After a few minutes' reflection he pressed the button, and at once a wave line, traced in ink, appeared on a narrow white fabric band, the latter resembling a telegraph recorder tape.

The band which moved rapidly, was unrolled from one reel and rolled up on another. Whenever the inventor wished to "write" down his thoughts, he would press the button, which started the mechanism as well as the recording tracer.

(Below is shown the record of a Menograph, the piece of tape being actual size.

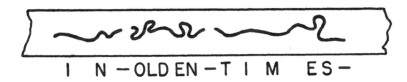

I N −OLD EN −T I M ES −

Where the wave line breaks, a new word or sentence commences; the three words shown are the result of the thought which expresses itself in the words, *"In olden times."* . . .)

The Menograph was one of Ralph 124C 41 +'s earliest inventions, and entirely superseded the pen and pencil.

It was only necessary to press the button when an idea was to be recorded and to release the button when one reflected and did not wish the thought-words recorded.

Instead of writing a letter, one sent the recorded *Meno-tape*, and inasmuch as the Menolphabet was universal and could be read by anyone—children being taught it at an early age—it was considered that this invention of Ralph's was one of his greatest gifts to humanity: Twenty times as much work could be done by means of the Menograph as could be done by the old-fashioned writing, which required considerable physical effort. Typewriters soon disappeared after its invention. Nor was there any use for stenographers, as the thoughts were written down direct on the tape, which was sent out as a letter was sent centuries ago.

As was his custom in the evening he worked for some hours in the laboratory, and retired at midnight. Before he fell asleep he attached to his head a double leather head-band with metal temple plates, similar to the one used in connection with the Menograph.

He then called for his man, Peter, and told him to "put on" Homer's *Odyssey* for the night.

Peter went down to the library on the 15th floor, and took down from a shelf a narrow box, labeled *Odyssey, Homer*. From this he extracted a large but thin reel on which was wound a long narrow film. This film was entirely black but for a white transparent waveline running through the center of it.

Peter returning to Ralph's bedroom placed the reel containing the film in a rack and introduced the end of the film into the *Hypnobioscope*. This wonderful instrument, invented by Ralph, transmitted the impulses of the wave-

49

line direct to the brain of the sleeping inventor, who thus was made to "dream" the *Odyssey.*

It had been known for centuries that the brain could be affected during sleep by certain processes. Thus one could be forced to dream that a heavy object was lying on one's chest, if such an object was placed on the sleeper's chest. Or one could be forced to dream that one's hand was being burnt or frozen, simply by heating or cooling the sleeper's hand.

It remained to Ralph, however, to perfect the Hypnobioscope, which transmitted words direct to the sleeping brain, in such a manner that everything could be remembered in detail the next morning.

This was made possible by having the impulses *act directly and steadily on the brain.* In other words, it was the Menograph reversed, with certain additions.

Thus, while in a passive state, the mind absorbed the impressions quite readily and mechanically and a story "read" by means of the Hypnobioscope left a much stronger impression than if the same story had been read while conscious.

For thousands of years humanity had wasted half of its life during sleep—the negative life. Since Ralph's invention, all this was changed. Not one night was lost by anyone if anywhere possible, conditions permitting. All books were read while one slept. *Most of the studying was done while one slept.* Some people mastered ten languages, during their sleep-life. Children who could not be successfully taught in school during their hours of consciousness, became good scholars if the lessons were repeated during their sleep-life.

The morning "newspapers" were transmitted to the

sleeping subscribers by wire at about 5 a. m. The great newspaper offices had hundreds of Hypnobioscopes in operation, the subscriber's wire leading to them. The newspaper office, notified by each subscriber what kind of news is desirable, furnished only such news. Consequently, when the subscriber woke up for breakfast he already knew the latest news, and could discuss it with his family, the members of which were also connected with the newspaper Hypnobioscope.

3

DEAD OR ALIVE?

AN APOLOGETIC COUGH came through the entrance to the laboratory. It was nearing one o'clock of the following day.

Several minutes later it was repeated, to the intense annoyance of the scientist, who had left orders that he was not to be interrupted in his work under any circumstances.

At the third "ahem!" he raised his head and stared fixedly at the empty space between the doorjambs. The most determined optimist could not have spelled welcome in that look.

Peter, advancing his neck around the corner until one eye met that of his master, withdrew it hastily.

"Well, what is it?" came from the laboratory, in an irritated harsh voice.

Peter, in the act of retreating on tiptoe, turned, and once more cocked a solitary eye around the door-jamb. This one feature had the beseeching look of a dog trying to convey by his expression that not for worlds would he have got in the way of your boot.

"Beg pardon, sir, but there's a young—"

"Won't see him!"

"But, sir, it's a young lady—"

"I'm busy, get out!"

Peter gulped desperately. "The young lady from—"

At this moment Ralph pressed a button nearby, an electromagnet acted, and a heavy plate glass door slid down from above, almost brushing Peter's melancholy countenance, terminating the conversation summarily.

Having secured himself against further interruption Ralph returned to the large glass box over which he had been working, and in which one could see, through greenish vapors, a dog, across whose heart was strapped a flat glass box filled with a metal-like substance.

The substance in the box was Radium-K. Radium, which had been known for centuries, had the curious property of giving out heat for thousands of years without disintegrating and without apparently obtaining energy from any outside source.

In 2009, Anatole M610 B9, the great French physicist, found that Radium obtained all its energy from the ether of space and proved that Radium was one of the few substances having a very strong affinity for the ether. Radium, he found, attracted the ether violently and the latter surging back and forward through the Radium became charged electrically, presenting all the other well known phenomena.

Anatole M610 B9 compared the action of Radium on the ether with that of a magnet acting upon a piece of iron. He proved this theory by examining a piece of pure metallic Radium in an etherless space, whereupon it lost all its characteristics and acted like a piece of ordinary metal.

Radium-K, as used by Ralph, was not pure Radium, but an alloy composed of Radium and Argonium. This alloy

53

exhibited all the usual phenomena of pure Radium and produced great heat, but did not create burns on animal tissue. It could be handled freely and without danger.

The dog lying in the glass box had been "dead" for three years. Just three years previous, in the presence of twenty noted scientists Ralph 124C 41 + had exhibited a live dog and had proceeded to drain off *all* its blood till the dog was pronounced quite dead and its heart had stopped beating. Thereupon he had refilled the empty blood vessels of the animal with a weak solution of Radium-K bromide, and the large artery through which the solution was pumped into the body had been closed.

The flat box containing Radium-K was then strapped over the dog's heart and it was placed in the large glass case. The latter was filled with *Permagatol,* a green gas having the property of preserving animal tissue permanently and indefinitely. The purpose of the box containing Radium-K was to keep the temperature of the dog's body at a fixed point.

After the case was completely filled with gas, the glass cover was sealed in such a manner that it was impossible to open the case without breaking the seals. The scientists had agreed to return after a lapse of three years to witness the opening of the box.

There were several delicate instruments inside the box and these were connected by means of wires to recording instruments on the side, and these Ralph inspected twice each day. Throughout the three years the "dead" dog had never stirred a muscle. His temperature had not varied 1/100 of a degree and his respiratory functions had shown no signs of life. To all intents and purposes the dog was "dead."

The time was close at hand for the final stages of what Ralph considered to be his greatest experiment. Three years ago when he faced his fellow scientists at the end of the first stage of this work, he electrified them by announcing that he expected to prove that this dog, which they had all pronounced "dead," could be restored to life, unharmed, unchanged, with no more effects upon the dog's spirits, habits, and nature, than had the animal taken but a short nap.

For three years this experiment of Ralph 124C 41 + had been the subject of innumerable scientific papers, had been discussed intermittently in the newspapers and the date of the final phase of the great experiment was fixed in the mind of every human being on the planet.

If the experiment succeeded it meant the prolongation of human life over greater periods of the earth's history than had ever been possible. It meant that premature death except through accident would be ended.

Would he succeed? Had he attempted the impossible? Was he challenging Nature to a combat only to be worsted?

These thoughts obtruded themselves into his consciousness as he began the preparations for the great test of the afternoon. He pumped out the Permagatol from the box until the green vapor had completely disappeared. With infinite care he then forced a small quantity of oxygen into the box. The instruments recording the action of the respiratory organs indicated that the oxygen reaching the dog's lungs had stimulated respiration.

This being all he could do for the present, he pressed the button that raised the glass barrier, and summoned Peter by means of another button.

That individual, looking a trifle more melancholy than usual, responded at once.

"Well, my boy," said Ralph good-humoredly, "the stage is all set for the experiment that will set the whole world by the ears.—But you don't look happy, Peter. What's troubling your dear old soul?"

Peter, whose feelings had evidently been lacerated when the door had been lowered in his face, replied with heavy dignity.

"Beg pardon, sir, but the young lady is still waiting."

"What young lady?" asked Ralph.

"The young lady from Switzerland, sir."

"The—which?"

"The young lady from Switzerland, sir, and her father, sir. They've been waiting half an hour."

If a bomb had exploded that instant Ralph could not have been more astounded.

"She's here—and you didn't call me? Peter, there are times when I am tempted to throw you out—"

"Pardon sir," replied Peter firmly, "I made bold to assume that you might be interested in the young lady's arrival, and presumed to step into the laboratory to so inform—"

But his master had gone, shedding his laboratory smock as he went. Peter, gathering his dignity about him as a garment, reached the doorway in time to see the elevator slide downwards out of sight.

And in it, Ralph, his heart thumping in a most undignified way, was acting more like a schoolboy than a master of science. He twitched at his tie with one hand and smoothed his hair with the other, peering into the elevator's little mirror anxiously. Discovering a smudge on his cheek he checked the car between floors while he wiped away the spot with his handkerchief.

When he reached the reception room he sprang from the elevator eagerly and hurried in. Seated by one of the windows were Alice 212B 423 and her father. Both turned as he entered, and the girl rose to her feet and with a charming gesture held out both hands.

"We just *had* to come," she said prettily, and in perfect English. "You didn't give us an opportunity to thank you yesterday, and anyhow, we felt that telephot thanks were not nearly so nice. That is, father thought we really ought to come in person—of course, I did, too. I wanted to see you ever so much"—she broke off, and then, realizing the implication of her words, went on hastily with reddened cheeks and downcast eyes, "I mean, to—to thank you, you know."

"It was wonderful of you," he declared still holding her two hands, and utterly unmindful of the fact that she was gently trying to disengage them. Indeed, he was not conscious of anyone or anything but her, until the voice of her father brought him to the realization that there was someone else in the room.

"We need no introduction I think," said the gentleman, "but I am James 212B 422 and I must ask you to pardon our intrusion upon a busy scientist's time, but I felt that we should come personally to thank you for the great service you have done us both. She is my one daughter, sir, and I love her dearly—dearly—"

"I can quite understand that," said Ralph with an unconscious ardor that caused Alice, who had completely recovered from her momentary confusion, to dimple and blush delightfully.

57

"I'm afraid, father dear," she said, "that we are keeping a busy man too long. Your man," she added, turning to Ralph, "said you were engaged in a wonderful experiment, and could not be disturbed."

"Busy? Not at all," said Ralph gracelessly. "You should not have been kept waiting one moment, and I am very indignant with Peter for not breaking down the door. He should have known, when he saw you, that you were not to wait."

"Oh, please, don't scold him because of me," said Alice, not, however, at all displeased with the implied compliment.

"I didn't know yesterday that you spoke English," he said, "so I used the language-rectifier, but I see that you speak it perfectly. That is a great relief to me, I assure you, for I speak French very indifferently. But tell me," he continued, "how did you get here so soon? The afternoon transatlantic aeroliner is not due yet, and it can hardly be twenty-four hours since you left Switzerland."

"We had the honor of being the first passengers to arrive by means of the new *Subatlantic Tube*," said James 212B 422. "As you are doubtless aware, the regular passenger service opens next week, but being one of the consulting engineers of the new electromagnetic tube, my daughter and I were permitted to make the first trip westward. We made it in perfect safety, although it was a little risky, as some small portions of the tube are not entirely completed."

"And we were so anxious to get here as quickly as possible," broke in Alice with a glance at Ralph.

"But you shouldn't have risked your lives, in an untested tube," he exclaimed. And then, the scientist in him to the front: "Tell me all about this new tube. Busy with my own work I have not followed its progress closely enough to know all its details."

"It has been most interesting work," said James 212B 422, "and we regard it as quite an achievement in electrical engineering. The new tube runs in a straight line between New York and Brest, France. If the tube were to run straight along the bottom of the ocean the distance between the two points would be from 3600 to 3700 miles due to the curvature of the earth. For this reason the tube was pushed *straight through the earth*, thereby making the distance only 3470 miles.

"You will understand it better by examining this chart," and unfolding a plan, he proceeded to elaborate on the finer points of the tube construction. "The greatest trouble," he went on, "our engineers experienced near the middle of the tube; this point is 450 miles nearer the center of the earth and the heat became very marked. It was necessary to install large liquid-air plants at several points in the tube to reduce the heat, and now as you ride through no heat is noticed.

"We boarded the spacious steel car, which resembles a thick cigar, at Brest last night at midnight, and arrived at the New York terminal at noon today. There was only one stop, a few hundred miles out from Brest, because of several short-circuited electromagnets.

"There are no wheels to the tube car and it is propelled by magnetism only. At each three hundred feet is stationed a powerful tubular electromagnet, about thirty feet long, through which the tube car passes. Each electromagnet exerts a tremendous pull upon the car three hundred feet away, this being the only steel object, and the

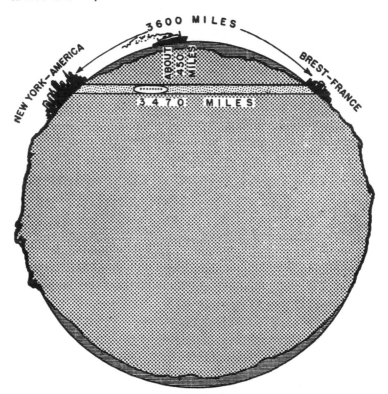

car rushes toward the electromagnet with a tremendous speed. When the car is only two feet away from this electromagnet, the current is cut off automatically by the car itself, the latter plunging through the open space of the magnet coil, only to be influenced now by the next electromagnet, three hundred feet distant.

"The momentum acquired by the pull of the former electromagnet propels the car with ever-increasing speed, and by the time it has passed through twenty-five electromagnets it has reached the speed of three hundred miles an hour. It then continues at a steady pace till the end of the journey.

"As the car is held suspended entirely by magnetism, there is practically no friction whatever, as there are no wheels or rails. The only friction is from the air, and in order that this may not heat the car it is equipped with a double wall, the space between the inner and outer walls being a vacuum. Consequently the temperature inside is comfortable at all times. Once inside the car, we retired and slept as soundly as in our swinging beds at home. There were no shocks, no noise, no rocking—all in all the trip was so delightful, that I must say the new tube is a decided success!"

"Fine, fine," said Ralph enthusiastically. "This new tube is going to revolutionize intercontinental travel. I suppose it won't be long now before we will regard our tedious twenty-four hour journeys as things of the past. Tell me," turning to Alice who had been an interested listener, "how did the trip impress you?"

"Oh," she exclaimed eagerly, "it was delightful! *So* smooth and fast! I was *so* excited. Really, it was over too soon."

As she spoke Ralph watched her with keen interest. Here was a girl who attracted him. Beneath the vivacity that so fascinated him he sensed the strength of her character, and the depth of her mind.

"I am so glad to be in New York," she was saying. "Do you know, this is my first visit here for ages. Why, the last time I can just barely remember, I was such a little girl. Father has been promising me a trip for years," with a laughingly reproachful glance at him, "but it took an avalanche to get us started."

61

"I'm afraid I've been a neglectful father of late years," said her father, "but my work has kept me tied pretty close to home. I, too, am pleased to be here once more, and my visit promises to be doubly interesting, for I understand that your great dog experiment will be completed today. I am looking forward to receiving the earliest reports of it at the hotel."

"But I can't permit you to spend your days here in a hotel," protested Ralph. "Of course you must both be my guests. Yes, yes," as they seemed about to demur, "I won't take no for an answer. I am counting on showing you New York, and, as for my experiment, it will give me great pleasure to have you both present in my laboratory this afternoon at four."

He pressed a button. "Peter will show you to your rooms, and I will send some one for your luggage."

"You are more than kind," said James. "This is quite unexpected, but none the less delightful. As to attending the meeting in your laboratory this afternoon, it is an honor, sir, that I appreciate deeply."

At this moment Peter stepped from the elevator and Ralph, after giving him instructions to show his guests to their apartment, and directions as to their bags, escorted them to the car and returned to the laboratory.

Promptly at four, Ralph greeted a notable group of fellow scientists, who had come from all corners of the planet to witness the completion of the famous "Dead-Alive Dog" experiment. A host of reporters lined the walls. Alice and her father were seated near Ralph.

A number of the twenty scientists who had witnessed

the beginning of the experiment three years before were dubiously contemplating the glass box, and one or two of the reporters, unawed by the personages in the laboratory, seven of whom were "Plus" men, seemed to find much covert amusement in the whole affair.

Finally, when all of the preparations were completed, and Ralph's two assistants had stationed themselves beside the glass box containing the body, the young scientist addressed the gathering.

"Ladies and gentlemen," he said, "you have come here to witness the final phase of my dog experiment. The preliminary phases you observed three years ago this day in this room. The seals you put in place are intact, and you may see them for yourselves, untouched as you left them.

"As I explained three years ago I formulated the theory that a well preserved animal, though dead to all intents and purposes, could be revived, or new life given to it, provided the body had not undergone decomposition; and also provided that none of the organs had suffered in the least.

"I found that the rare gas Permagatol would conserve animal tissue and animal organs indefinitely; when it is used in conjunction with a weak solution of Radium-K bromide, mixed with antiseptic salts, no part of an animal body would undergo any change for many years.

"I also found that the body would have to be kept at a fixed temperature and this was possible by the use of Radium-K alloy. I am now ready to prove my theory."

He signaled to his assistants, and with their aid, the seals were broken and the glass cover of the case removed.

A profound silence prevailed. Every eye was focussed on the dog and many of those present found it difficult to remain seated.

Ralph coolly and deliberately freed the dog of his bandages and attachments and placed him on an operating table in plain view of everyone.

From then on he and his aides moved rapidly. First the dead dog's artery was opened and the Radium-K bromide solution drained off. A young goat was brought in and strapped on the table, and in a very few seconds one of its arteries had been opened and connected to the dead dog's main artery. In less than a minute the dog's body was full of fresh warm blood and immediately efforts were made to bring the dog back to life.

Oxygen was freely administered and the heart was artificially pulsated by means of an electrical vibratory apparatus.

At the same time one of the assistants had trained a vacuum tube on the dog's head and its cathode shot the powerful F-9-Rays into the animal's brain. No sooner had these rays, which are among the most powerful brain stimulants, been trained on the dog than he began to show weak signs of life. One of the hind legs was drawn up with a jerk as if in a fit. Then came a faint heave of the chest, followed by a weak attempt to breathe.

A few minutes later the body seemed to contract and a shiver ran through it from head to tail. A deep respiration followed, and the animal opened its eyes as if awakening from a long sleep.

In a few minutes more the dog was lying on its paws and licking up milk when Ralph turned to the group and said:

"Gentlemen, the experiment is concluded and I believe the condition of the animal at this moment establishes sufficient proof of my theory."

As the reporters eagerly dashed from the laboratory to get to the nearest Telephot in order to communicate the news to the waiting world the scientists gathered around Ralph and one of them, a white haired old man considered to be the dean of the "Plus" men, voiced the sentiment of the entire group.

"Ralph, this is one of the greatest gifts that science has brought to humanity. For what you have done with a dog, you can do with a human being. I only regret for myself that you had not lived and conducted this experiment when I was a young man, that I might have, from time to time, lived in suspended animation from century to century, and from generation to generation as it will now be possible for human beings to do."

The vista opened up by the results of this experiment in the minds of the other scientists had dazed them and it was with the most perfunctory good-byes that they left the scene of the experiment, enveloped with their thoughts of the future.

Tired and exhausted by the nervous strain of the afternoon Ralph, a few minutes later, lay down on his bed for a few hours' rest. But as he closed his eyes there came to him a vivid picture of a pair of warm dark eyes, radiating admiration, trust and something more that aroused an emotion he had never before experienced.

4

FERNAND

ON THE FOLLOWING MORNING, Ralph, breakfasting alone, sent Peter to the apartments of his guests to ascertain at what hour they would be ready to do a little sight-seeing with him as guide.

He himself, in the habit of rising at an early hour, had not expected to see either Alice or her father much before noon, and it was a decided surprise to him, to see the latter enter the room a moment after Peter had gone on his errand.

"I see that you, too, like to get up with the birds," said the scientist after they had exchanged morning greetings.

"And Alice also, when she is at home; but the journey, and our exciting day following it have tired her. I shall just have a bite to eat with you, if you will permit me, and then I must be off to keep an appointment with one of the chief engineers of the Tube."

"Then you will be unable to accompany us on our tour of the city?"

"Yes, but don't let that interfere with your plans. I know that Alice will be safe with you," smiled her father, "and I daresay you young people can get along very well without me."

"I'm sorry," replied Ralph, but in his heart he could not but rejoice that he was to spend the day alone with her who, in a few short hours had so captivated him. Perhaps something of this showed in his face, for James 212B 422 smiled to himself.

Peter returned and presently Ralph and James were seated together at the table. They conversed in a more or less desultory manner until just before the end of the meal when Alice's father, laying down his napkin, said:

"Before I leave you I have a request to make, a strange one, you may think." He hesitated. "A short time ago I said that I felt that Alice would be safe in your care. I had a special reason for making the remark. The fact is, I am a little worried about her. A young man, by name Fernand 600 10, has been making rather a nuisance of himself lately. He has asked her to marry him, a number of times, and she has refused, and he has begun to force his attentions on her in a manner which savors something of persecution.

"In fact, he went so far, four days ago, as to threaten her. Exactly what passed between them I don't know, but I do know that, although she treated the matter lightly at the time, she is frightened. I have an impression that he may try to kidnap her if she does not accept him, and though, in these enlightened days such a thing seems ridiculous—well, the affair makes me a little nervous myself. When we left Switzerland I understood that he was there, but he may have followed Alice here. If he has and renews his unpleasant surveillance I shall know that my fears have some grounds."

"What does this Fernand look like?" asked Ralph.

"Oh, a nice looking fellow—at least, the women think

so. Personally, I don't care for him. He is tall and dark, and has the sort of temperament that seems to delight in opposition. His eyes have a sullen expression, and his mouth is somewhat weak. She has, by the way, another admirer, a thoroughly harmless chap, who is here on a visit at present. He is the Martian Llysanorh' CK 1618, and he is really hopelessly infatuated, but being, as I say, a very decent chap who respects the law against marriage between the Martians and Terrestrials, he has never annoyed her in any way. On the other hand they are very good friends, and I doubt very much whether she even suspects that he has any other feeling for her than that of a devoted friend."

As he was speaking, a picture leapt to Ralph's mind. He saw again two faces, each in the center of a Telephot, who, among the crowds of applauding admirers regarded him with such intentness. If these were the two men who cared for Alice, each in his own way, it was not surprising that they had displayed more than a passing interest in the man who had rescued her from what seemed to be certain death, and who was a possible rival.

He recounted the incident to James, who agreed with him that in all likelihood his suspicions were correct, and the two men parted for the day, the older bearing with him the comforting reassurance that Ralph would take care of his daughter as he would himself.

It was nearing eleven when Alice appeared, bright-eyed after her long rest. She laughingly apologized for being so late, and they set out at once.

"You know," he said before they started, "we New Yorkers are strange birds. We only like our city when we are far away from it, or when we can take some stranger about to show him or her the marvels of the town. As a matter of fact the real, dyed-in-the-wool New Yorker hates the town and only stays in it because it has cast a spell over him which he cannot escape."

By this time they had arrived at the street level of the building and Ralph bade Alice sit down on a chair in the vestibule. He pressed a nearby button twice and a servant brought two pairs of what appeared to be roller-skates.

In reality they were *Tele-motor-coasters*. They were made of alomagnesium and each weighed only about one and one-half pounds. Each had three small, rubber-covered wheels, one in front and two in the rear. Between the wheels was a small electric motor—about the size of a lemon; this motor could only be operated by high frequency currents and, despite its small size, could deliver about one-quarter horsepower.

Ralph explained the coasters and their use to his companion; and after they had put them on by means of an ingenious clutch, whereby the coaster could be snapped onto the shoe in less than five seconds, they both went out into the street. From each coaster a thin insulated wire led up the wearer's back to the hat or cap. Here it was attached to the *collector*, which was a stiff pin about eight inches long, projecting half-way out from the hat or cap. This pin sucked up, as it were, the high frequency electricity and carried it to the small motors, which latter propelled the coaster. To control the speed of the motor, one simply lifted up the front part of the coaster; this not only cut off the current, but automatically braked the two rear wheels.

When the two rolled out in the street, Alice at once remarked upon the splendid condition of the roads.

"You see," the scientist explained, "for centuries the city had to content itself with temporary pavements, until about fifty years ago it woke up and covered every street with steelonium.

"You will notice that there are no cracks or fissures. Steelonium won't rust and is ten times as strong as steel. We now make our streets by putting down large slabs of the metal, six inches thick. After they are in place we weld them together electrically and the result is a perfect street composed of a uniform sheet of metal without cracks or breaks; no dirt or germs can collect. The sidewalks are made in the same manner.

"As a matter of fact, the Tele-motor-coasters would not be possible were it not for the metallic streets. The flat spring which trails on the street between the two rear wheels must make continuous contact with the metallic 'ground,' else the current cannot flow."

"But where does the current come from?" asked the girl.

"You have perhaps noticed already the white slender posts at the edge of the sidewalk, and on their tops umbrella-like insulators which carry a thick spiked wire. This wire, as you see, is about fifteen feet above the curb and carries the high frequency current which not only supplies our coasters with power, by way of our needle collectors, but also propels all the vehicles which you see gliding so noiselessly."

They were well under way and rolled along at a speed of about twenty miles an hour. They passed thousands of citizens, all coasting at high speed. There was no noise but the peculiar hum produced by the thousands of motors, a sound which was in nowise annoying.

Each sidewalk was divided in two parts. On the outside only people going in one direction, on the inside only people going in the opposite direction could coast. Collisions, therefore, were impossible. If a person rolling on the outside wished to enter a store, it was necessary to go to the end of the block, and then turn to the left, which brought him on the inside of the sidewalk where he could roll up to his destination. Of course, this was only necessary when the sidewalk was crowded, nothing preventing one's crossing it if but few people were on the block.

The trolley car had long since become obsolete as well as the gasoline-driven automobile. Only electromobiles carrying either passengers or freight were to be seen. Each vehicle was equipped with a short collector mast by means of which the electrical energy was conveyed to the motors. The wheels of all vehicles were rubber-covered. This accomplished two purposes: one to insulate the vehicle from the metallic street, the other to minimize the noise to the greatest extent.

Although Alice had had a good scientific training, some of the wonders of New York amazed her and she, as strangers had done for centuries, asked questions continuously, while her companion eagerly explained everything with a pleasure peculiar to the New Yorker, loving his town.

"What are those strange spiral wire affairs hanging high over all street crossings?" was one of her first questions.

"Those illuminate our streets at night," was the answer. "They are iridium wire spirals, about ten meters in diameter, hanging forty meters up in the air, at the intersection of all our streets. This evening you will see how the entire spiral will glow in a pure white light which is absolutely cold. The wire throws out the light, and after sundown you will find that the streets will be almost as light as they are now. Each spiral furnishes over one-half million candlepower, consequently one is needed only where streets intersect, except on very long blocks, when a smaller spiral is hung in the middle."

Presently, while crossing a large square they passed Meteoro-Tower No. 26, of the seventh district, and Ralph at once launched off into praise of it.

"While you of other countries have a good weather service, we in New York boast of having the finest climate of any town on the face of the globe. As you may imagine, our weather-engineers always have difficult work, owing to the peculiar shape of the city, geographically as well as physically. The tall spires and buildings make the work exceptionally hard, as the air currents are extremely erratic over the city and very hard to control. We now have sixty-eight Meteoro-Towers, all of various power, in Consolidated New York. These are scattered over a radius of ninety miles from the *City Governor's Building*, and control the weather as well as the temperature of New York's two hundred million inhabitants.

"You may look at a thermometer any time during the year and you will find it invariably pointing at fifty units.* There is never an excess of humidity in our air and life is made enjoyable for the hard-working city dwellers, thanks to our well-trained weather engineer corps.

"During the daytime rain or snow is unheard of. There is continuous sunshine during the three hundred and

* 72° Fahrenheit.

sixty-five days of the year. Between two and three each morning it rains for exactly one hour. This is done to freshen the air and to carry the dust away. It is the only rain New York ever gets and it seems to be sufficient for all purposes."

When it neared noon Ralph escorted his companion to a luxurious eating place, which across its entrance bore the name *Scienticafé*. "This is one of our best restaurants, and I think you will prefer it to the old-fashioned masticating places," he told her.

As they entered, a deliciously perfumed, yet invigorating fragrance greeted them.

They proceeded at once to the *Appetizer*, which was a large room, hermetically closed, in which sat several hundred people, reading or talking.

The two sat down on leather-upholstered chairs and looked at a humorous daily magazine which was projected upon a white wall, the pages of the magazine changing from time to time.

They had been in the room but a few minutes when Alice exclaimed:

"I am ravenously hungry and I was not hungry at all when we entered. What kind of a trick is it?"

"This is the Appetizer," Ralph exclaimed laughing, "the air in here is invigorating, being charged with several harmless gases for the purpose of giving you an appetite before you eat—hence its name!"

Both then proceeded to the main eating salon, which was beautifully decorated in white and gold. There were no attendants and no waiters, and the salon was very quiet except for a muffled, far-off, murmuring music.

They then sat down at a table on which were mounted complicated silver boards with odd buttons and pushes and slides. There was such a board for each patron. From the top of the board a flexible tube hung down to which one fastened a silver mouthpiece, that one took out of a disinfecting solution, attached to the board. The bill of fare was engraved in the board and there was a pointer which one moved up and down the various food items and stopped in front of the one selected. The silver mouthpiece was then placed in the mouth and one pressed upon a red button. The liquid food which one selected would then begin to flow into the mouth, its rate of speed controlled by the red button. If spices, salt or pepper were wanted, there was a button for each one which merely had to be pressed till the food was as palatable as wanted. Another button controlled the temperature of the food.

Meats, vegetables, and other eatables, were all liquefied and were prepared with utmost skill to make them palatable. When changing from one food to another the flexible tube, including the mouthpiece, were rinsed out with hot water, but the water did not flow out of the mouthpiece. The opening of the latter closed automatically during the rinsing and opened as soon as the process was terminated.

While eating they reclined in the comfortably upholstered leather arm-chair. They did not have to use knife and fork, as was the custom in former centuries. Eating had become a pleasure.

"Do you know," said Ralph, "it took people a long time to accept the scientific restaurants.

"At first they did not succeed. Humanity had been masticating for thousands of years and it was hard to overcome the inherited habit.

"However, people soon found out that scientific foods prepared in a palatable manner in liquid form were not only far more digestible and better for the stomach, but they also did away almost entirely with indigestion, dyspepsia, and other ills, and people began to get stronger and more vigorous.

"The scientific restaurants furnished only foods which were nourishing and no dishes hard to digest could be had at all. Therein lay the success of the new idea.

"People at first did not favor the idea because the new way of eating did not seem as aesthetic as the old and seemed also at first devoid of the pleasures of the old way of eating. They regarded it with a suspicion similar to a 20th century European observing a Chinaman using his chopsticks. This aversion, however, soon wore off as people became used to the new mode of eating, and it is thought that the close of the century will witness the closing of all old-fashioned restaurants.

"You will notice, however, that the liquid scientific foods are not absolutely liquid. Some of them, especially meats, have been prepared in such a manner that slight mastication is always necessary. This naturally does away with the monotony of swallowing liquids all the time and makes the food more desirable."

After their luncheon Ralph and Alice rolled "uptown," the former explaining the various sights as they progressed. At Broadway and 389th street, in a large square, a petrified animal stood upon a pedestal. The girl, desiring to know what it represented, approached and read this inscription, hewn in the stone:

> PETE
>
> The last Horse in Harness in the
> Streets of New York
> Died on this Spot
> June 19th, 2096 A. D.

"The poor thing," she said, "it looks so pitiful, doesn't it? To think that once the poor dumb animals were made to labor! It is much better nowadays with electricity doing all the work."

Ralph smiled at this very feminine remark. It was like her, he thought tenderly, to feel sympathy for even this former beast of burden.

As they turned to leave the pedestal, the girl made an involuntary shrinking movement toward him. He looked up and saw, advancing toward them on Tele-motor-coasters, a tall dark man, a little younger than himself. The newcomer ignoring Ralph utterly, rolled up to Alice.

"So you are enjoying the sights of New York," he said, with no other greeting, and with a disagreeable smile on his lips.

"Yes," said the girl coldly, "I *was* enjoying them, very much."

He bit his under lip in an annoyed fashion, and a dull flush mounted to his hair. "I told you I'd follow you if you ran away," he said in a lower tone.

Ralph, unable to catch the words, but reading a menace in the fellow's look, stepped forward. Alice turned to him eagerly and put her hand on his arm.

"What is next on our program, Ralph?" she asked in a

clear voice, while at the same time she pressed his wrist with her fingers as a signal for him to go on.

As if Fernand had not existed, she moved away, her hand still on Ralph's arm. "Please, please," she murmured as he would have turned back.

"That fellow needs his head punched," muttered Ralph savagely.

"Don't make a scene—I just couldn't bear it," she pleaded. Looking down at her he saw that she was on the verge of tears.

"I'm sorry," he said gently.

"I'm so ashamed," she said pathetically, "what must you think!"

"That I should go back and knock his head off," said Ralph. "But if you ask me not to, I won't. I suppose that was Fernand?"

She looked at him in astonishment. "Do *you* know him?"

"Your father told me."

"Oh," she said, troubled, "father shouldn't have done that. But I suppose he was afraid of a meeting of this sort."

"How long has he been following you around?"

"Oh, for ages, it seems. Really, about a year. I never liked him, but lately he's been perfectly horrid, and acts in such a threatening way—you saw him. I can't see why he should take the trouble to annoy anyone who loathes him as I do. But let's forget it. We have had such a wonderful day that I don't want it spoiled." And then timidly, with downcast eyes: "I called you Ralph. You must have thought me very forward, but I wanted him to think—"

She stopped suddenly, and in confusion. And then, her

natural gaiety coming to her rescue: "Heavens, the more I say, the worse I make it, don't I?"

"It sounded fine to me," said Ralph, falling in with her mood, "I hope you will always call me that."

And laughing together they rolled on.

5

NEW YORK A.D. 2660

BEING MUCH INTERESTED in sports, she desired to know presently how the modern New Yorker kept himself in condition and for his answer Ralph stopped at a corner and they entered a tall, flat-roofed building. They took off their coasters, stepped into the electromagnetic elevator and ascended the fifty odd stories in a few seconds. At the top, they found a large expanse on which were stationed dozens of flyers of all sizes. There was a continuous bustle of departing and arriving aerial flyers and of people alighting and departing.

As soon as Ralph and Alice appeared a dozen voices began to call: *"Aerocab, sir, Aerocab, this way please!"* Ralph, ignoring them, walked over to a two-seated flyer and assisted his companion to the seat; he then seated himself and said briefly to the "driver," *"National Playgrounds."* The machine, which was very light and operated entirely by electricity, was built of metal throughout; it shot up into the air with terrific speed and then took a northeasterly direction at a rate of ten miles per minute, or 600 miles per hour.

From the great height at which they were flying it was not hard to point out the most interesting structures, towers, bridges, and wonders of construction deemed impossible several centuries ago.

In less than ten minutes they had arrived at the National Playgrounds. They alighted on an immense platform and Ralph, leading Alice to the edge, where they could see the entire playgrounds, said:

"These National Playgrounds were built by the city in 2490, at the extreme eastern end of what used to be Long Island, a few miles from Montauk.* An immense area had been fitted up for all kinds of sports, terrestrial and aquatic as well as aerial. These municipal playgrounds are the finest in the world and represent one of New York's greatest achievements. The City Government supplied all the various sport paraphernalia and every citizen has the right to use it, by applying to the lieutenants in charge of the various sections.

"There are playgrounds for the young as well as for the old, grounds for men, grounds for the women, grounds for babies to romp about in. There are hundreds of baseball fields, thousands of tennis courts, and uncounted football fields and golf links. It never rains, it is never too hot, it is never too cold. The grounds are open every day in the year, from seven in the morning till eleven at night. After sunset, the grounds and fields are lighted by thousands of iridium wire spirals, for those who have to work in the daytime.

"As a matter of fact all the great baseball, tennis, and football contests are held after sundown. The reason is apparent. During the daytime, with the sun shining, there is always one team which has an advantage over the other, on account of the light being in their eyes. In the evening, however, with the powerful, stationary light

* Since this was written a national playground has actually been created at Montauk, L. I. A rather strange coincidence.

overhead, each team has the same conditions and the game can be played more fairly and more accurately." *

Ralph and his companion strolled about the immense grounds watching the players and it was not long before he discovered that she, like himself, was enthusiastic about tennis. He asked her if she would care to play a game with him and she acquiesced eagerly.

They walked over to the dressing building where Ralph kept his own sport clothes. Since the girl had no tennis shoes, he secured a pair for her in the Arcade, and they sauntered over to one of the courts.

In the game that followed, Ralph, an expert at tennis, was too engrossed in the girl to watch his game. Consequently, he was beaten from start to finish. He did not see the ball, and scarcely noticed the net. His eyes were constantly on Alice, who, indeed, made a remarkably pretty picture. She flung herself enthusiastically into her game, as she did with everything else that interested her. She was the true sport-lover, caring little whether she won or not, loving the game for the game itself.

Her lovely face was flushed with the exercise, and her hair curled into damp little rings, lying against her neck and cheeks in soft clusters. Her eyes, always bright, shone like stars. Now and again they met Ralph's in gay triumph as she encountered a difficult ball.

He had never imagined that anyone could be so graceful. Her lithe and flexible figure was seen to its best advantage in this game requiring great agility.

Ralph, under this bombardment of charms, was spellbound. He played mechanically, and, it must be admitted,

* At the time this was written, no illuminated, night time sports fields existed.

wretchedly. And he was so thoroughly and abjectly in love that he did not care. To him, but one thing mattered. He knew that unless he could have Alice life itself would not matter to him.

He felt that he would gladly have lost a hundred games when she at last flung down her racket, crying happily: "Oh, I won, I won, didn't I?"

"You certainly did," he cried. "You were wonderful!"

"I'm a little bit afraid you let me win," she pouted. "It really wasn't fair of you."

"You were fine," he declared. "I was hopelessly outclassed from the beginning. You have no idea how beautiful you were," he went on, impulsively. "More beautiful than I ever dreamed anyone could be."

Before his ardent eyes she drew back a little, half pleased, half frightened, and not a little confused.

Sensing her embarrassment he instantly became matter-of-fact.

"Now," he said, "I am going to show you the source of New York's light and power."

A few minutes later, after both had changed their shoes, they were again seated in an aerocab and a twenty minute journey brought them well into the center of what was formerly New York state.

They alighted on an immense plain on which twelve monstrous Meteoro-Towers, each 1,500 feet high, were stationed. These towers formed a hexagon inside of which were the immense *Helio-Dynamophores*, or Sun-power-generators.

The entire expanse, twenty kilometers square, was covered with glass. Underneath the heavy plate glass squares were the photo-electric elements which transformed the solar heat *direct* into electric energy.

The photo-electric elements, of which there were 400 to each square meter, were placed in large movable metal cases, each case containing 1,600 photo-electric units.

Each metal case in turn was movable, and mounted on a kind of large tripod in such a manner that each case from sunrise to sunset presented its glass plate directly to the sun. The rays of the sun, consequently, struck the photo-electric elements always vertically, never obliquely. A small electric motor inside of the tripod moved the metal case so as to keep the plates always facing the sun.

In order that one case might not take away the light from the one directly behind it, all cases were arranged in long rows, each sufficiently far away from the one preceding it. Thus shadows from one row could not fall on the row behind it.

At sunrise, all cases would be almost vertical, but at this time very little current was generated. One hour after sunrise, the plant was working to its full capacity; by noon all cases would be in a horizontal position, and by sunset, they again would be in an almost vertical position, in the opposite direction, however, from that of the morning. The plant would work at its full capacity until one hour before sunset.

Each case generated about one hundred and twenty kilowatts almost as long as the sun was shining, and it is easily understood what an enormous power the entire plant could generate. In fact, this plant supplied all the power, light, and heat for entire New York. One-half of the plant was for day use, while the other half during daytime charged the chemical gas-accumulators for night use.

In 1909 Cove of Massachusetts invented a thermo-electric Sun-power-generator which could deliver ten volts and six amperes, or one-sixtieth kilowatt in a space of twelve square feet. Since that time inventors by the score had busied themselves to perfect solar generators, but it was not until the year 2469 that the Italian 63A 1243 invented the photo-electric cell, which revolutionized the entire electrical industry. This Italian discovered that by derivatives of the Radium-M class, in conjunction with Tellurium and Arcturium, a photo-electric element could be produced which was strongly affected by the sun's ultra-violet rays and in this condition was able to transform heat *direct* into electrical energy, without losses of any kind.

After watching the enormous power plant for a time Alice remarked:

"We, of course, have similar plants across the water but I have never seen anything of such magnitude. It is really colossal. But what gives the sky above such a peculiar black tint?"

"In order not to suffer too great losses from atmospheric disturbances," Ralph explained, "the twelve giant Meteoro-Towers which you notice are working with full power as long as the plant is in operation. Thus a partial vacuum is produced above the plant and the air consequently is very thin. As air ordinarily absorbs an immense amount of heat, it goes without saying that the Helio-Dynamophore plant obtains an immensely greater amount of heat when the air above is very clear and thin. In the morning the towers direct their energy toward the East in order to clear the atmosphere to a certain extent, and in the afternoon their energy is directed toward the West for the same purpose. For this reason, this plant furnishes fully thirty per cent more energy than others working in ordinary atmosphere."

As it was growing late they returned to the city, traversing the distance to Ralph's home in less than ten minutes.

Alice's father arrived a few minutes later, and she told him of the delightful time she had had in the company of their distinguished host.

Shortly after they had dined that evening Ralph took his guests down to his *Tele-Theater*. This large room had a shallow stage at one end, with proscenium arch and curtain, such as had been in use during the whole history of the drama. At the rear of the room were scattered a number of big upholstered chairs.

When they had seated themselves, Ralph gave Alice a directory of the plays and operas that were being presented that night.

"Oh, I see they are playing the French comic opera, *La Normande,* at the National Opera tonight," she exclaimed. "I have heard and read much of it. I should like to hear it so much."

"With the greatest of pleasure," Ralph replied. "In fact, I have not heard it myself. My laboratory has kept me so busy, that I have missed the Opera several times already. There are only two performances a week now."

He walked over to a large switchboard from which hung numerous cords and plugs. He inserted one of the plugs into a hole labeled "National Opera." He then manipulated several levers and switches and seated himself again with his guests.

In a moment, a gong sounded, and the lights were

gradually dimmed. Immediately afterward, the orchestra began the overture.

A great number of loud-speaking telephones were arranged near the stage, and the acoustics were so good that it was hard to realize that the music originated four miles away at the National Opera House.

When the overture was over, the curtain rose on the first act. Directly behind it several hundred especially constructed Telephots were arranged in such a manner as to fill out the entire space of the shallow stage. These telephots were connected in series and were all joined together so cleverly that no break or joint was visible in the rear part of the stage. The result was that all objects on the distant stage of the National Opera were projected full size on the composite Telephot plates on the Tele-Theater stage. The illusion was so perfect in all respects that it was extremely hard to imagine that the actors on the Telephot stage were not real flesh and blood. Each voice could be heard clearly and distinctly, because the transmitters were close to the actors at all times and it was not necessary to strain the ear to catch any passages.

Between the acts Ralph explained that each New York playhouse now had over 200,000 subscribers and it was as easy for the Berlin and Paris subscribers to hear and see the play as for the New York subscriber. On the other hand, he admitted that the Paris and Berlin as well as the London playhouses had a large number of subscribers, local as well as long distance, but New York's subscription list was by far the largest.

"Can you imagine," mused Alice, "how the people in former centuries must have been inconvenienced when they wished to enjoy a play? I was reading only the other day how they had to prepare themselves for the theater hours ahead of time. They had to get dressed especially for the occasion and even went so far as to have different clothes in which to attend theaters or operas. And then they had to ride or perhaps walk to the playhouse itself. Then the poor things, if they did not happen to like the production, had either to sit all through it or else go home. They probably would have rejoiced at the ease of our Tele-Theaters, where we can switch from one play to another in five seconds, until we find the one that suits us best.

"Nor could their sick people enjoy themselves seeing a play, as we can now. I know when I broke my ankle a year ago, I actually lived in the Tele-Theater. I cannot imagine how I could have dragged through those dreary six weeks in bed without a new play each night. Life must have been dreadful in those days!"

"Yes, you are right," Ralph said. "Neither could they have imagined in their wildest dreams the spectacle I witnessed a few days ago.

"I happened to be passing this room and I heard such uproarious laughter that I decided to see what caused it all. Entering unnoticed, I found my ten-year-old nephew 'entertaining' half-a-dozen of his friends. The little rascal had plugged into a matinee performance of 'Romeo and Juliet' playing at the 'Broadway'—in English of course. He then plugged in at the same time into *Der Spitzbub*, a farce playing that evening in Berlin, and to this, for good measure, he added *Rigoletto* in Italian, playing at the 'Gala' in Milan.

"The effect was of course horrible. Most of the time, nothing but a Babel of voices and music could be heard;

but once in a while a single voice broke through the din, followed immediately by another one in a different language. The funniest incident was when, at the 'Broadway,' Juliet called: *Romeo, Romeo, where art thou, Romeo?*, and a heavy comedian at the Berlin Theatre howled: *Mir ist's Wurst, schlagt ihn tot!*

"Of course, everything on the stage was blurred most of the time, but once in a while extremely ludicrous combinations resulted between some of the actors at the various theaters, which were greeted with an uproar by the youngsters."

As he concluded the anecdote the curtain rose once more, and the audience of three settled back to enjoy the second act of the opera.

Later, when it was all over, they went down to the street floor at Ralph's suggestion, where they put on their Tele-motor-coasters, preparatory to seeing more of New York—this time by night.

The party proceeded to roll down Broadway, the historic thoroughfare of New York. Despite the fact that it was 11 o'clock at night, the streets were almost as light as at noonday. They were illuminated brilliantly by the iridium spirals, hanging high above the crossings. These spirals gave forth a pure, dazzling-white light of the same quality as sunlight. This light moreover was absolutely cold, as all electrical energy was transformed into light, none being lost in heat. Not a street was dark—not even the smallest alley.

James 212B 422, as well as his daughter, lingered over the superb displays in the various stores and they entered several to make a few purchases. Alice was much impressed with the automatic-electric packing machines.

The clerk making the sale placed the purchased articles on a metal platform. He then pushed several buttons on a small switchboard, which operated the "size" apparatus to obtain the dimensions of the package. After the last button was pressed, the platform rose about two feet, till it disappeared into a large metal, box-like contrivance. In about ten to fifteen seconds it came down again bearing on its surface a neat white box with a handle at the top, *all in one piece*. The box was not fastened with any strings or tape, but was folded in an ingenious manner so that it could not open of its own accord. Moreover, it was made of *Alohydrolium*, which is the lightest of all metals, being one-eighth the weight of aluminum.

The automatic packing machine could pack anything from a small package a few inches square up to a box two feet high by three feet long. It made the box to suit the size of the final package, placed the articles together, packed them into the box which was not yet finished, folded the box after the handle had been stamped out, stenciled the firm's name on two sides and delivered it completely packed, all within ten to fifteen seconds.

The box could either be taken by the purchaser or the clerk would stencil the customer's name and address into the handle, place a triangular packet-post stamp on the box and drop it into a chute beside the counter. It was carried down into the *Packet-Post Conveyor*, which was from seventy-five to one hundred feet below the level of the street, where it landed on a belt-like arrangement moving at the rate of five miles an hour. The action was entirely automatic and the chute was arranged with an automatic shutter which would only open when there was no package immediately below on the moving belt. This precluded the possibility of packages tumbling on top of each other and in this way blocking the conveyor tube.

When the package had landed on the conveyor belt it traveled to the nearest *distributor office*, where the post office clerk would take it from the belt and see if it was franked correctly. The stamp was then machine cancelled and after the clerk had noted the address he routed it to the sub-station nearest to the addressee's home. Next he clamped onto the package an automatic metal "rider" which was of a certain height, irrespective of the size of the package.

The package with its rider was placed on an express conveyor belt traveling at the rate of 25 miles an hour. This express belt, bearing the package, moved at an even speed, and never stopping, passed numerous sub-stations on the way. At the correct sub-station the rider came against a contact device stretching across the belt at right angles, at a certain height. This contact arrangement closed the circuit of a powerful electromagnet placed in the same line with the contact, a few feet away from the express belt. The electromagnet acted immediately on the metal package (Alohydrolium is a magnetic metal), drawing it in a flash into the sub-station from the belt. If there was another package right behind the one so drawn out, it was handled in the same manner.

After the package had arrived at the sub-station it was despatched to its final destination. Another rider was attached to it and the package placed on a local conveyor belt passing by the house to which it was addressed. On arriving at the correct address its rider would strike the contact overhead, which operated the electromagnet, pulling the package into the basement of the house, where it fell on the platform of an electric dumb-waiter. The dumb-waiter started upward automatically and the package was delivered at once.

By this method a package could be delivered in the average space of forty minutes from the time of purchase. Some packages could be delivered in a much shorter time and others which had to travel to the city limits took much longer.

"How wonderful!" Alice exclaimed after Ralph had explained the system. "It must have taken decades to build such a stupendous system."

"No, not quite," was the reply. "It was built gradually by an enormous number of workers. The tubes are even now extended almost daily to keep pace with the growth of the city."

From the stores Ralph took his guests to the roof of an aerocab stand and they boarded a fast flyer.

"Take us about 10,000 feet up," Ralph instructed the driver.

"You haven't much time," the man answered, "at 12 o'clock all cabs must be out of the air."

"Why?"

"Today is the 15th of September, the night of the aerial carnival, and it's against the law to go up over New York until it's all over. You have twenty-five minutes left, however, if you wish to go up."

"I forgot all about this aerial carnival," said Ralph, "but twenty-five minutes will be time enough for us if you speed up your machine."

The aerial flyer rose quickly and silently. The objects below seemed to shrink in size and within three minutes the light became fainter.

In ten minutes an altitude of twelve thousand feet had been reached, and as it became too cold, Ralph motioned to the driver not to rise further.

The spectacle below them was indescribably beautiful. As far as the eye could see was a broad expanse studded with lights, like a carpet embroidered with diamonds. Thousands of aerial craft, their powerful searchlights sweeping the skies, moved silently through the night, and once in a while an immense transatlantic aerial liner would swish by at a tremendous speed.

Most beautiful of all, as well as wonderful, were the *Signalizers.* Ralph pointed them out to his guests, saying:

"In the first period of aerial navigation large electric lamps forming figures and letters were placed on house-tops and in open fields that the aerial craft above might better find their destinations. To the traffic flying 5,000 feet or higher such signals were wholly inadequate, as they could not be correctly read at such a distance. Hence the signalizers. These are powerful searchlights of the most advanced type, mounted on special buildings. They are trained skyward and shoot a powerful shaft of light directly upward. No aerial craft is allowed to cross these light shafts. Each shaft gives a different signal; thus the signalizer in Herald Square is first white; in ten seconds it changes to red and in another ten seconds it becomes yellow. Even an aerial liner at sea can recognize the signal and steer directly into the Herald Square pier, without being obliged to hover over the city in search of it. Some signalizers have only one color, flashing from time to time. Others more important use two searchlights at one time, like the one at Sandy Hook. This signalizer has two light shafts, one green and one red; these do not change colors, nor do they light periodically."

From on high Ralph's guests marveled at these signalizers, which pierced the darkness all around them. It was a wonderful sight and the weird beauty of the colored shafts thrilled Alice immeasurably.

"Oh, it is like a Fairyland," she exclaimed. "I could watch it forever."

But presently the aerocab was descending rapidly and in a few minutes the strong light from below had obliterated the light shafts. As the craft drew closer the streets could be seen extending for miles like white ribbons and the brilliantly lighted squares stood out prominently. They landed, at the stroke of twelve, and Ralph found three unoccupied chairs on the top of one of the public buildings and only then did they notice that hundreds of people were seated, watching the sky expectantly.

At the last stroke of twelve, all the lights below went out and simultaneously the light shafts of all the searchlights. Everything was plunged in an utter darkness.

Suddenly overhead at a great height the flag of the United States in immense proportions was seen. It was composed of 6,000 flyers, all together in the same horizontal plane. Each flyer was equipped with very powerful lights on the bottom, some white, some red, others blue. Thus an immense flag in its natural colors was formed and so precisely did the flyers co-operate that, although they all were at least 50 feet from each other, the appearance to those below was that of an unbroken silk flag, illuminated by a searchlight. The immense flag began to move. It passed slowly overhead, describing a large circle, so that the entire population below obtained a perfect view.

Everyone applauded the demonstration. Then as suddenly as it had appeared the flag vanished and all was once more in darkness. Ralph explained to his guests that the lights of each one of the aerial flyers had been shut off simultaneously in preparation for the next spectacle.

All at once there was seen an enormous colored circle which revolved with great rapidity, becoming smaller and smaller, as though it were shrinking. Finally it became a colored disc, whirling rapidly on its axis. In a few seconds, the edge opened and a straight line shot out, the disc unrolling like a tape measure. After a few minutes more, there remained nothing of the disc. It had resolved itself into a perfectly straight many-hued line, miles long. Then the lights went out again. The next spectacle was a demonstration of the solar system. In the center a large sun was seen standing still. Next to the "sun" a small red round globe spun rapidly about it, representing the planet Mercury. Around both the sun and the "planet" Mercury revolved another globe, blue in color; this was Venus. Then followed a white orb, the "Earth" with the moon turning about it. Next came the red planet Mars with its two small moons, then green Jupiter and its moons, and Saturn in yellow. Uranus was orange and lastly came Neptune in pink, all globes and their moons traveling in their proper orbits around the "sun." * While the spectacle was in progress a white "comet" with a long tail traveled across the paths of the planets, turned a sharp corner around the "sun," its tail always pointing away from that body, recrossed the orbits of the "planets" again on the other side and lost itself in the darkness.

Several other spectacles were presented, each more su-

* In 1911 the outer planet Pluto had as yet not been discovered.

perb than the one preceding it. The carnival closed with a light-picture of the Planet Governor. This was exhibited for fully five minutes during which time the applause was continuous.

"We have never seen such a marvelous spectacle," James 212B 422 declared. "You Americans still lead the world. Upon my word, the old saying that 'Nothing is impossible in America,' still holds good."

It was after one when they reached the house, and Ralph suggested a light lunch before they retired for what remained of the night. The others assented and Ralph led the way to the *Bacillatorium*.

The Bacillatorium, invented in 2509 by the Swede 1A 299, was a small room, the walls and bottom of which were composed of lead. On each of the four sides were large vacuum bulbs on pedestals. These tubes, a foot in height and about six inches thick and two feet in diameter, were each equipped with a large concave Radioarcturium cathode. The glass of the tube in front of the cathode had a double wall, the space between being filled with helium gas.

The rays emanating from the cathode, when the tube was energized with high oscillatory currents, were called *Arcturium Rays* and would instantly destroy any bacilli exposed to them for a few seconds. Arcturium Rays, like X-rays, pass through solid objects, and when used alone burned the tissue of the human body. It was found, however, that by filtering arcturium rays through helium no burns would result, but any germ or bacillus in or on the body would be killed at once.

The Bacillatorium was prescribed by law and each citizen ordered to use it at least every other day, thus making it impossible for the human body to develop contagious diseases. As late as the 20th century more than half the mortality was directly attributable to diseases communicated by germs or bacilli.

The Bacillatorium eradicated such diseases. The arcturium rays, moreover, had a highly beneficial effect on animal tissue and the enforced use of the Bacillatorium extended the span of human life to between one hundred and twenty and one hundred and forty years, where in former centuries three score and ten was the average.

6

"GIVE US FOOD"

THE FOLLOWING DAY was set aside for a visit to the Accelerated Plant Growing Farms. It had been known for hundreds of years that certain plants, such as mushrooms, could be fully developed in a few days. Plant or vegetables grown under glass and the temperature within kept at a high point, would grow at great speed and be ready for the market long before those grown in the open.

But only recently, as Ralph explained to Alice, had it been possible to do this on a large scale. To be sure, certain vegetables, like asparagus, lettuce, peas, etc., had been produced in hothouses for hundreds of years, but these, after all, were rather luxuries, and could not be classed as essentials.

When, about the year 2600, the population of the planet had increased tremendously and famines due to lack of such essentials as bread and potatoes had broken out in many parts of the world, it was found vitally necessary to produce such necessities on a larger scale and with unfailing regularity. These farms became known under the term of Accelerated Plant Growing Farms and were located in every part of the world. The first (and now obsolete) European and African farms were built along the lines of the old-fashioned hothouses. The European farms were simply horizontal steel-latticed roofs, with ordinary glass panes, permitting the sunlight to penetrate to the soil beneath. While covering huge acreages, they were not heated artificially, using only the sun's rays to accelerate plant growth. As compared with Nature's single crop of wheat or corn, two could be made to grow in the same season by means of these super hothouses.

Similar farms were used in America until Ralph undertook their study and approached the subject from a scientific angle. One of his first efforts was to obtain greater heat for these huge hothouses. One of these hothouses is about three miles long and the same width. Ralph took the existing hothouses, which were simply oblong steel and glass boxes, and built a second hothouse box covering each of them, thus creating a double-walled, air-locked hothouse. The second glass-paneled wall was about two feet inside the outer one. This left dead air locked between the walls, and as air is a poor heat conductor, the heat in the hothouse was retained longer, particularly during a cold night.

Ralph and Alice left early in the morning, winging their way in an aeroflyer toward northern New York, where there were many Accelerated Plant Growing Farms. When the farms came into view, the entire country below, so far as the eye could see, appeared to be dotted with the glass-covered roofs of the plants, reflecting the sunlight and affording an unusual sight. Alice marveled at their number, for while she had seen some of these farms in Europe, she had never seen so many grouped together of such immensity.

Within a few minutes, they landed near one of the giant hothouses. The manager led them inside of the farm labeled No. D1569.

D1569 was exclusively a wheat growing farm. Where Mother Nature used to grow one crop of wheat a year, Ralph's latest Accelerator made it possible to grow four, and sometimes five crops a year. In the old-fashioned European farms such as Alice knew, only two crops could be grown.

"How is it possible," she asked, "that you can obtain three more crops a year than we do in Europe?"

"In the first place," said Ralph, "it may be taken as an axiom that the more heat you supply to plant growth, the quicker it will grow. Cold and chilly winds retard plant growth. Electricity and certain chemicals increase the ratio of growth, a fact that has been known for many centuries. It is, however, the scientific application of this knowledge that makes it possible to raise five crops a year. The European farms use only the heat of the sun to stimulate plant growth, but during the night, when the temperature drops, growth is practically nil.

"Notice that the top and sides of our hothouses have two walls. In other words, one hothouse is built within another. The air locked between the two hothouses is an excellent heat insulator and even though the sun is low at 4 o'clock, the temperature is practically unchanged in the hothouse, at 8 or 9 o'clock in the evening. Even in the winter, when the sun sets about 4 o'clock and it is cold, we are able to store up enough heat during the day to keep a high temperature as late as 7 and 8 o'clock. If we did nothing between the hours of 8 in the evening and 8 in the morning, the temperature would continue to fall to a point where no plant growth would be possible.

"Here in America we had to have a greater production to supply our huge population. It was a pure case of necessity. So we had to employ artificial heating during the night.

"If we start sinking a shaft into the earth, the heat increases rapidly as we go down—more quickly in some parts of the world than others. On an average, the temperature rises about one degree Fahrenheit each 100 feet of depth. We found it economic, therefore, to use the earth's own heat to heat our farms.

"By means of high speed drills, we can cut a three-foot shaft 3,000 feet deep in the earth in less than a month. We go down until we strike a temperature around 100 to 120 degrees Fahrenheit. Then we lower steel tanks into the cavity and run pipes up to the surface. The tanks are filled with water and two larger pipes run from each tank into the circulating system of pipes, around the lower walls throughout the length and breadth of the farms. The shafts are then closed at the top and we have a circulating system that is both cheap and efficient. The hot water continually rises into the pipes and circulates. As it cools, it flows down again into the tanks, where it is reheated and rises again. Thus the temperature of our farms is uniform all the year around and plant growth is as rapid during the night as during the day.

"Heat alone, however, is not sufficient. We should still get only a normal growth. We wanted five crops a year. I put my research forces to work studying fertilizers. While the old nitrogen fertilizers were excellent, they were not suitable for high pressure, high speed growing methods. We evolved chemicals which were both cheap and easy to apply. We found that small quantities of *Termidon,* when mixed with water and sprayed over the field by overhead sprayers, which you will see running along the ceiling, would accelerate the growth of the crops enormously.

"This liquid Termidon is sprayed over the entire length and breadth of the field before planting time, so that the soil becomes well soaked. The Termidon immediately turns the soil into a rich, dark strata, the best soil for potatoes, wheat, or corn. No other fertilizer need be used, the Termidon, applied after every growth, giving the soil all the vitality necessary."

They were now in the field, when suddenly Alice asked:

"What is the peculiar tingling in the soles of my feet, I feel as we walk along? You are using some electrical vibrations, I suppose."

"You guessed correctly," Ralph replied. "With all our artifice the speed of the plant growth had not been accelerated sufficiently. I therefore insulated the inside hothouse from the ground. The inside hothouse rests upon glass blocks, and is electrified by high frequency currents. The entire area is sprayed day and night with a high frequency current, in the use of which we found was the real secret of driving plant growth ahead at enormous speed. The theory of course is nothing new, having been known for centuries. What is new, however, is the way it is done. It makes all the difference in the world if the current density is too high or too low, if it is direct or alternating current, and many other details. I found that the quickest way to accelerate plant growth by electricity was to send the current from the growing plant toward the ceiling, and the current must be direct, pulsating, but not alternating."

Ralph asked for a discharge pole from one of the attendants. It was a metal pole about seven and a half feet high. In the middle it had a long glass handle which Ralph grasped. He then set the pole vertically so that its top was about six inches from the glass ceiling. A roar of fine sparks leaped from the steel frame of the ceiling to the top of the pole.

"See," said Ralph, "there is the current we use in accelerating the growth of our plants."

Removing the pole, Ralph continued: "The electrical current density per square foot is not very high and the wheat does not get a very great amount of electricity during the twenty-four hours. *The continuance of the force applied is what counts.*"

After luncheon, during which they ate some of the bread made from wheat grown on the premises, they went to an adjoining farm, also a wheat farm, where harvesting was in full progress. Machinery, suspended from overhead tracks, cut the wheat rapidly with circular scythes. All the wheat being of the same height, the machine cut the wheat almost directly below the heads, dropped them on a conveyor, which carried the real harvest to a central distribution point. Another machine immediately followed the cutter, grasping the stalks that were still standing, unerringly *pulled out the straw hulks*, roots and all. Thus the roots were entirely removed and the soil loosened, obviating plowing. Within a few hours following cutting, the last stem was out. The field was then sprayed with the liquid Termidon from overhead. Within another three hours, sowing began, also from overhead pipes.

Going to an adjoining plant, they saw a bare field with almost black soil, ready to be sowed. An attendant, at Ralph's request, pulled a switch and immediately Alice witnessed a seed rain from the overhead pipes.

"The seed," Ralph explained, "is supplied to these tubes by means of compressed air. The tubes are perforated, and when air pressure is applied, the seed, flowing through the tubes is ejected evenly—just so many seeds to a given area. Closing the openings of the pipes automatically as the seeding proceeds, means only a given quantity of seed will fall upon any given square foot of soil. This makes for scientific planting, and we raise just the exact quantity of wheat we want."

Alice watched the seed rain spellbound. Like a wall of rain it slowly receded into the distance until finally it disappeared. "How long does it take to sow this field?" she asked.

"From two to three hours, depending upon the size of the field. This particular field is about eight miles long and three miles wide. The process should be completed within about three and a half hours."

"And when will this crop be ready for the harvest?" Alice wanted to know.

"In about seventy days from now the wheat will be ready to cut."

Alice walked along thoughtfully and then inquired whether the great cost of such an undertaking would not make the growing of the foodstuffs prohibitive.

"Quite the contrary," Ralph replied. "We are now growing wheat, corn, potatoes, and many other foodstuffs, for a much lower price than our ancestors did five or six hundred years ago. You see, it is the installation of the hothouses and machinery that is costly, but these glass and steel buildings will last for centuries with proper care. The frames are made of non-rusting steel which needs no painting. The glass lasts for hundreds of years. The labor we use in planting and harvesting is a mere fraction of what was used in olden times. Thus, for sowing and harvesting this plant, eight by three miles, we require only twenty people. This is a very much smaller number than was used on a small old-fashioned farm.

"We waste nothing. We have no poor crops, and we get three or four times as much as our ancestors did."

They stepped up to a glass case containing samples of wheat grown for hundreds of years, showing that a head of wheat grown in the year 1900 was about three inches long, while the present year's crop showed a length of more than six inches, or twice as much flour content per stalk. Ralph also pointed out to Alice that the modern wheat stalk was much bigger in circumference than the ancient ones, which, he explained, was attributable to the greater weight of the modern wheat. The old stalks could not possibly have supported such a great weight of grain, so it was necessary to cultivate bigger stalks.

Ralph went on: "As I said before, we waste nothing here. The harvested hulks go to a paper mill, a few miles away, and are converted into a first class paper. A few decades ago an entirely new paper process was invented. Where straw was once used for making so-called strawboard or cardboard, the finest commercial papers are now being made from the straw grown right here. We no longer annihilate our forests, to make paper pulp. Since the invention of the straw paper process, chopping trees for paper purposes has been forbidden and all the paper in this country is now made exclusively of straw chemically treated."

A potato farm was seen the same afternoon. The processes in this and other vegetable growing plants being under somewhat different conditions than the wheat farm.

It was dark when Alice and Ralph returned to wheat farm No. D1569, and found that the manager of the plant had prepared an elaborate supper for the two, informing Alice that *everything* set before her had been grown the same day. The whole wheat bread had been harvested that morning, the grains had been artificially aged by heat, flour had been made, and the bread had just been baked. He said, somewhat proudly, that this was probably a record.

The entire meal consisted of vegetables, all grown in plants in the vicinity. There were fresh peas, fresh asparagus, new potatoes, fresh lettuce, juicy apples, and many delicacies.

For dessert the manager brought in, on a great silver tray, a number of new crossfoods, which as yet had not been seen in the open market. There was, the *appear,* a cross between an apple and a pear, which had all the good qualities of the apple and all the good qualities of the pear. There was also a delightful combination of plum and cherry, a cantaloupe with a faint taste of orange, and cherries as big as a good-sized plum.

Tea was served from tea leaves grown in one of the farms and harvested the same day. The manager also showed Alice cigarettes and set before Ralph a box of cigars, made from tobacco planted and harvested that day. The leaves had been aged rapidly by dry heat in a partial vacuum.

Both thanked the manager for the novel treat. After dining they walked into the wheat growing farm. It was now dark outside, but in the hothouse, the wheat for miles and miles seemed to be aglow in a light purple haze. A faint half-crackling, half-swishing sound was heard. The points of the wheat seemed to be almost luminous.

"This is the night appearance of the electricity you felt this afternoon," said Ralph. "During the daytime you do not see the faint discharge, but in darkness it becomes luminous. One pole of the high frequency generator is connected with the soil and the other with the steel framework of the hothouse. Without this electric current we would not be able to grow more than two, or at the utmost, three crops a year.

"It is also necessary to vary the strength of the current during the day. With full sunshine and maximum heat we do not need as much current as we use during the night. Several hundred years ago when using somewhat similar methods that had not as yet been perfected, it was necessary to use artificial light during the night, as plants need light for growth. We found, however, that the electric current with the soft light which you see glowing now, is sufficient for the purpose and the plant does not require any other light."

Alice stood for many minutes silently watching the beautiful sight of the glowing purple field, listening to the faint crackling discharge of the electric current as it leaped from the points of the wheat into the air. They finally left and flew back to New York.

The next day, Ralph took Alice to one of the city's Synthetic Food Laboratories. While flying toward it, Ralph explained that while the farms which they had looked over yesterday were for the purpose of raising real foodstuffs, there were many commodities that could not be so raised, such as sugar, milk, and many others, which were now made synthetically. As chemists had known for many hundreds of years, sugar was nothing but a simple carbohydrate, whereas milk was composed of an emulsified mixture of casein, lactic acid, butter, water and minor constituents.

As the population increased, it was neither possible, nor profitable to obtain these foods by natural means, and it was found necessary to resort to the chemist.

They alighted at one of these chemical laboratories which manufactured sugar, milk, cooking fats, butter and cheese.

There was really not much to see, save large boiler-like chemical retorts, large white enameled vats, and a lot of pumps and electric motors. The manager explained that sugar was made out of sawdust and acids. The sawdust, he explained, was digested in the huge white enameled steel vats by means of certain acids. After the digesting process was completed other chemicals were added, the ensuing syrup then being run through retorts and finally emerging as a stream of white liquid sugar.

The manager handed Alice a piece of clear, transparent sugar, as well as several specimens of crystallized sugar, which she ate delightedly, exclaiming laughingly that "it was the best sawdust she had ever eaten."

They next visited the synthetic milk section, where hundreds of thousands of gallons of milk were produced every day. This being a recent discovery the manager explained it in detail.

"Milk," he said, "has been known since the dawn of humanity, but only when man became somewhat civilized did he learn how to obtain milk from animals, such as the goat and the cow. It took thousands of years to domesticate these animals, and it is not known at what period man first began to milk these domestic animals for his own supply of milk.

"Men of an inquisitive nature must have asked themselves the question for thousands of years, 'Why grow grass, let the cow eat the grass, digest it, and finally turn it into milk? Why not eliminate the cow entirely?' The thought, while elementary, had no actual basis or foundation for centuries, because the chemical processes of the intermediate stages between the grass and the final milk were too complicated and were not at all well understood. Only during the last few years has the problem been solved satisfactorily.

"Now we grow the fresh grass, which we put into these large retorts, where the grass is digested just the same as if it were in the stomach of the cow. By the addition of salts and chemicals we imitate this digestive process, and by eliminating solids and the liquids, we finally get a milk that is not only better than the original cow or goat milk, but has many qualities not possessed by cow's milk.

"Try this glass of artificial milk," he said to Alice, handing her a glass of rather unappetizing-looking liquid of a slightly pale green color, not too clean looking and somewhat thick. Alice tasted it, however, and found that it tasted exactly like a good rich cow's milk. The manager asked Alice to close her eyes and take a good drink. She did so, and exclaimed in surprise that it tasted exactly like rich, creamy milk.

The manager then explained that synthetic milk was free from the bacteria which give milk its white color. Moreover, the fat content was much higher than cow's milk, and, there being a greater percentage of sugar present, the milk tasted sweeter. Certain added salts gave it a distinguishing taste.

From this milk, he further explained, any sort of fat could be extracted, and the usual array of milk products, such as butter, all sorts of cheeses, etc., could be made much better than from cow's milk, which never ran uniform.

After inspecting the laboratory, Alice and Ralph sampled a number of products, all of which tasted excellent —better, if anything, than the natural products. The manager added "You will find our synthetic products are far easier to digest, and are more wholesome than the natural product. The reason is that we have eliminated all of the disease-carrying microbes and bacteria, retaining only the beneficial ones, which we can control very easily in our plants, more than the cow or goat can do."

7

THE END OF MONEY

A FEW DAYS LATER, Alice, while rolling along one of the elevated streets of the city with Ralph, inquired how the present monetary system had been evolved: "You know," she confided, "I know very little of economics."

"Well," said Ralph, "all monetary systems of the past or present are based on one principle—the exchange of one thing for another. At first it was simply a bartering or swapping of such things as a goat for a pig, or a string of beads for a piece of cloth. Only much later did money evolve. Before we had coins, certain rare shells were used as tokens. Still later, precious metal was exchanged for goods, using the weight of the metal as a basis. Later on, coins were developed, and still later on, paper money replaced part of the coins. Where the shells, the precious metals, and, later the metal coins, had intrinsic value, the paper money had no such value. The public accepted with faith and confidence a piece of paper across which was printed the guarantee that the bearer of it would receive so many metal dollars in exchange for the piece of paper. The paper money was built upon confidence that the people had in the government issuing the paper money.

"Very few people ever thought of going to a bank or to

the government's treasury to exchange the paper money for gold or silver coins. Instead, they freely circulated this paper money among themselves, and after people became accustomed to it, they accepted the paper money to the practical exclusion of gold and silver. Particularly in the former United States did this system reach a high development, more so than in old Europe, where paper money was used in conjunction with gold or silver coins.

"In the United States, however, nothing but paper money was eventually used, even to the exclusion of the smallest coins. Whereas up to a certain period the dollar bill was the smallest paper money unit used, this was later split into the former coins of fifty cents, twenty-five cents, ten cents, five cents, and one cent. It was found that small paper bills the size of former postage stamps were not very practical when issued in separate pieces, so the printed tape coins, which we have today, came into extensive use.

"The small metal box you carry, and from which you unroll your printed perforated tape, still represents the old paper money. When you, therefore, make a purchase today and you unroll fifty cents in ten cent denominations on your perforated roll, you are using a portion of the old system.

"But the real monetary system is built upon confidence. It could not be otherwise today because we have no more precious metals. When, about 95 years ago, the Frenchman P865 + finished the transmutation of all the precious metals, the death-knell of the old monetary system was sounded. Everybody could make gold and silver for less than iron used to cost in the old days. Consequently, if you had a one hundred dollar bill that said on its face that you could exchange it for one hundred dollars' worth of gold, you could have gone to the treasury and received five twenty dollar gold pieces, which, however, were not worth more, perhaps, than one or two cents. So of what use was the one hundred dollar bill? *

"When P865 + made his announcement, it caused neither panic nor confusion. Several centuries prior there would have been panic, but the world had been progressing in knowledge, and understood that commerce and economics are stabilized by confidence.

"There is only one thing in this world that has a real value, and that is man's work. You can replace almost everything else with something else, but you can not replace labor. The modern economic structure is, therefore, reared entirely upon man's work.

"When the check came into use, in the 19th century the monetary system underwent a great change. Instead of people paying what they owed by means of coins or banknotes, they took to paying each other by means of a written piece of paper—the check. Billions upon billions of dollars and cents changed hands, simply by signing a check to some one else, the check clearing through the bank. While one account was credited, another was debited. There was little actual money that changed hands, either between the man who wrote the check and the man who received it, or even between the banks who cleared the checks. In other words, this entire check system was based upon credit. You received a check for one hundred dollars from a man who owed you one hundred dollars. You took this check in good faith because you knew that

* When this was written gold coins were legal tender. Gold payments were outlawed by Congress in 1933.

112

he must have the one hundred dollars in the bank—otherwise he probably would not make out the check. You sent the check to your bank, which, in turn, collected it from the bank in which your debtor had his account. In all these transactions no real money ever changed hands. It was credit, pure and simple, all the way through.

"So when P865 + demonstrated his synthetic metals, the situation did not change at all. The people appreciated the fact that the government, in one way or another, must be good, and that although the money reserves as figured in metal dollars and cents had become valueless, every one knew that the country was not founded and based upon valueless metals alone. Incidentally, no government, the entire world over, could have redeemed in gold or silver coin all of its outstanding obligations.

"Therefore, when gold and silver became practically valueless, nothing happened, because actual coins were no longer used, and every one used checks, so that even banknotes had become obsolete.

"But, with the devaluation of the so-called 'precious' metals the governments substituted other values. This was done at first by setting fixed values on property, such as real estate, buildings, manufacturing plants, etc. Valuations of these were made several times a year, and whoever owned such properties was given a 'State-value certificate.' A building, valued at $50,000, was appraised by the state three or four times or more, a year, and a certificate was given to you which you took to your bank, the latter immediately crediting you with part of the $50,-000. If you wanted to sell your property to a friend for $50,000 or more, you would take his check and then, demand from your bank the return of the original deed, which in turn would be transferred to your friend. In that case your bank would credit you with the $50,000 check of your friend, while he would have the property.

"Of course the illustration which I gave is not exactly accurate, for the reason that you could not get from your bank the exact amount of the valuation of whatever realty changed hands. The bank advanced about seventy percent of the appraised value, with certain exceptions. This also was in no wise different from the way our ancestors were accustomed to do, because in the old days such a transaction would simply have been called a mortgage. The important difference, however, later on, was that the valuation was made by the state and such valuation was final. This tended to stabilize real estate and property valuations.

"Merchandise, today, is bought and sold the same as it was bought and sold centuries ago, and that is by check. So is everything else, including labor. Every workman is, of course, paid by check, which check he can use either in his own bank account or for buying merchandise from his grocer or tailor, getting the difference in a check or otherwise in fractional paper tape coin.

"These government paper tape coins and banknotes— the few that are being used—instead of being covered by gold and silver bullion, are now covered by real estate bonds or other tangible property."

"But," Alice asked, "suppose there were a panic, as described in some of the ancient books, and everybody ran to the bank at once to get his money, what would happen?"

"Nothing," said Ralph. "Absolutely nothing. Suppose there was a 'panic,' as you call it. In the first place, why should there be one? There is no reason for it and no one nowadays would think of running to the bank and getting his or her 'money.' There is no 'money,' as you call it.

"Remember, the banks are all under government control, and if a bank should fail, which no bank has done for the last four hundred years, the government would be obliged to make good the shortage out of its own resources. If everybody ran simultaneously to every bank throughout the country, a bank would simply make out a check for each total balance, and pass out a check for the amount. Then the next morning, as the people could not eat their checks for breakfast, they would have to do one of two things: either take the check back to the bank and redeposit it, or exchange the check for commodities.

"That means that within twenty-four hours all the checks would have found their way back to the banks and things would be just exactly where they had left off before the 'run' on the bank. As banks are no longer under the necessity of paying in coin or banknotes, but under the law can pay by check, there is no reason why any one should wish to make a 'run' on the bank, simply to get a check."

"But," Alice persisted, "suppose you draw out more than you have to your credit? Suppose you write out a check for more than you have in the bank? What happens then?"

"You probably can answer that just as well as I can," replied Ralph. "To do so is a prison offense, and again, it would do you no good, because following the first offense you would get a warning from the government, and at the second such offense you would get a still stronger warning, and on the third, you would go to jail, because the first two offenses could perhaps be mistakes, but the third could not. On top of this, your account would be withdrawn from all banks and you would not be able to open another account again for ten years, because all checks as you know, are identified with fingerprints in addition to the signature. The fingerprint experts of the government would prevent you from opening another account in any bank anywhere in the country. So no one abuses his checking privilege and writes out checks when there are no funds to his credit."

A few days later Ralph took Alice to one of the great industrial artificial cloth works. They flew to Pennsylvania, where the great artificial silk, cotton, and wool mills were located. Ralph explained that during the 20th century silk had finally been made artificially from wood and chemicals. This was then known as artificial silk. But only during the last century had it been possible to manufacture artificial cotton and artificial wool, synthetically from wood and other chemicals. Moreover, they wore better than real cotton and real wool.

In the enormous plant were immense tanks in which the raw materials were first cooked and then treated by chemicals until the fibers issued in fine microscopic streams from nozzles under hydraulic pressure, the threads were then wound on huge reels. From here the hanks were sent to the spinneries and cloth-weaving mills.

Of particular interest was the new kind of cloth, which was much lighter than wool or cotton, and, at the same time, cooler in summer and warmer in winter. This material was made from cork, which was first pulverized and then afterwards digested by means of chemicals. Under hydraulic pressure, a somewhat thick thread was obtained, which had all the good properties of cork, but none of its poor ones. This cork thread, when woven into cloth, made a texture both light and durable, had a velvety touch to the fingers, and being a poor heat conductor, protected the wearer from heat in the summer and cold in the winter.

A number of combinations were made whereby cork thread and silk thread were spun together, giving an entirely new product, with all the virtues of silk as well as those of cork.

8

THE MENACE OF THE INVISIBLE CLOAK

LEAVING the Pennsylvania mills the aeroflyer, traveling at high speed landed the party within a very short time on one of the tall landing buildings in New York. Ralph and Alice made their way down to the elevated roadway, where, at Ralph's suggestion they put on their *power skates,* for, as he explained smilingly, it was but a short distance to his home and the exercise would do them both good and give them an appetite for luncheon.

When they were but a little way from their destination Ralph became conscious of a faint hissing sound close behind them. Twice he glanced over his shoulder, but the roadway at that hour—it was just before noon—was deserted.

Yet the sibilant sound persisted, seeming to be getting closer and closer, like some persevering insect about to alight.

Alice apparently heard nothing, or perhaps she thought it merely one of the noises of the street, for she chattered on in the gay animated fashion that was one of her charms, oblivious to the fact that the man at her side was so preoccupied that he scarcely replied to her.

For Ralph had now satisfied himself that there was nothing anywhere around them which could cause that

118

untiring pursuant hiss. Then from what secret invisible source did it emanate—and why?

To the scientist, accustomed to explaining the unexplainable, it was ominous—menacing—

Again he turned to look behind him, along the deserted way, and at that moment he heard a stifled cry from the girl beside him. He whirled to face her, and faced—nothing! He was alone in the empty street!

Unbelieving, doubting the evidence of his eyes, he stared about him, too astounded for the moment, by this mystifying and amazing disappearance to think collectively.

Above him the sun shone in a clear blue sky, before and behind him stretched the still roadway. Then he was aware of the silence, the deadly quiet. For the hissing had receded into nothingness, and with it, Alice.

As the full force of the catastrophe struck him, something akin to panic seized him. Danger to himself he could have faced with the calm courage of a brave man, but this unseen and unexpected blow from an invisible source aimed at the girl so close and dear to his heart smote him with a chill terror that for an instant held him powerless in its grip.

That he should have been careless when she was in danger—but this was no time for self-reproaches. To act, and to act at once—that was vital.

Thoughts of high frequency radio waves—of X-rays—of Fernand—

"Fernand!" he exclaimed aloud, and with the name coherent thought returned. Putting on all possible speed he covered the distance to his home in a few seconds and dashed up to his laboratory, the while his swiftly-working brain attacked the greatest personal problem that it had ever been called upon to solve.

Having experimented with ultra-short waves, he knew that it was possible to create total transparency of any object if the object could be made to vibrate approximately at the same rate as light. He was familiar with the theory, and although he had worked on it at times, he had never seen a practical demonstration of it.* He realized a machine was in the hands of someone, intent on kidnapping Alice. He knew, too, that a police description would be flashed within a radius of thousands of miles instantly, it would be necessary for the abductor to keep Alice invisible for some time to come, for fear of some one seeing and recognizing her. All this flashed through his mind as he assembled a detecting apparatus consisting of a portable aerial and a small box containing a few radio instruments and a pair of headphones.

The aerial, by being rotated, could determine the point from which the waves emanated. In ten minutes Ralph had the apparatus rigged up and began rotating the aerial, until a roaring noise was heard in the telephones. He knew that this must be the apparatus producing the invisibility, and within a few seconds he had dashed from the house on his power skates, carrying the detector in front of him. Two of his assistants accompanied him.

The pursuit was on. As they approached the kidnapper the sounds in the telephones became stronger. They sped along Broadway, while the hastily notified police kept the way open. The rising sound in the 'phones clearly indi-

* In 1925 John L. Reinartz, working with ultra-short radio waves, actually made it possible to look through solid metal plates with the naked eye.

cated they were headed directly toward the abductor.

They gained steadily on him while the rolling, flying police cleared Ralph's way with their shrieking sirens, while the kidnapper had to pick his way slowly through crowds.

The chase led them into a narrow street on the outskirts of the city.

The sound that came through the telephones was now exceedingly loud, indicating that the quarry was near by. But this very nearness was confusing to Ralph, for the volume of sound prevented him from exactly locating the invisible kidnapper and the girl. In vain he turned the aerial in all directions, seeking one point from which it came louder than another that would determine the course of his pursuit. For the moment he was halted, and, like some hound baffled by the cunning of the fox, he cast about him eagerly, waiting for what he knew must come, the next move of the pursued man.

And then it came—a deepening tone in the telephones, a gradation of sound that to the trained ear of the scientist told him all that he wished to know. With an exultant cry he sprang forward, and dashed through the entrance of a small store.

The proprietor, whose state of mind may best be described by the word "flabbergasted," struggled for some moments in vain for speech while Ralph and his men, with outstretched hands eagerly swept from wall to wall.

"Here, here, you fellows," he finally managed to gasp, "what are you after? What are you trying to do? You'll knock something over in a minute. Hey, look out there— there it goes!"

For Ralph had reached around a tailor's dummy,

knocking it over as his hands closed upon something behind it, something invisible and yet warm and firm; something that quivered and shrunk away at his touch.

The proprietor, rushing forward to pick up the dummy, stopped short, gaping. Ralph's hands, at the moment of contact, vanished into thin air. But in an instant they reappeared, as he drew towards him, out of the influence of the ultra-short waves what he knew must be the bound and gagged form of Alice.

Once away from the influence of the apparatus she became visible again. A sack had been tied over her head and shoulders and her hands were tightly bound to her sides. She was still on her roller skates, and her feet had been left free, the sack being sufficient to render her almost wholly helpless, and unable to make any effective resistance.

As Ralph removed the fastenings and released her, she staggered and clung to him, her head dropping in exhaustion.

"Oh," she gasped faintly, "what is it? Where did you go?"

"Water!" exclaimed Ralph harshly to those about him, and the fat storekeeper, trembling with excitement, but withal displaying an extraordinary energy for one who could never at any time have been a streamline model, made a dive for a vase of flowers on the counter. Grasping the tops of the flowers with one hand he flung them in a corner, and tendered the vase of discolored water to Ralph, panting the while as one who has run his race, and emerged triumphant.

"I said water—not mud," shouted Ralph in exasperation,

as he rubbed the girl's cold hands between his own warm ones.

"Well, that's water, ain't it?" said the man, and Ralph glowered at him.

"Please," said Alice, trying to withdraw her hands, "I'm all right, indeed I am. I was just a little dizzy for a minute, but it has all passed now."

The color returned to her pale cheeks with a rush, and she straightened herself, and turned away in some confusion, her hands instinctively going to her hair, the gesture that women have ever used when at a loss for words.

In the meantime, Ralph's two assistants had found the ultra-wave machine by the very simple method of feeling about the spot where the girl had been discovered. When their hands disappeared they knew that they had it, and Ralph ordered some water thrown upon it, which had the twofold result of stopping its activity and of bringing it into view.

Having assured himself that Alice was unharmed and recovering from the shock resulting from her misadventure, the scientist made a minute examination of the instrument. It was a complicated machine and one totally strange to him. As he studied it he felt a growing conviction that this was no earth-made machine, but one conceived and made by a Martian. Undoubtedly it was the work of some master of science, a true mental giant.

Then where, he asked himself, did Fernand—if it was Fernand—secure it, and how? His object, of course, was obvious. He was evidently prepared to go to any lengths to secure the girl for himself. Had he not so threatened her? His method of attack had been ingenious—fiendishly ingenious. Here was no mean antagonist, no petty enemy, but one whose cunning would tax Ralph's resourcefulness to the utmost.

When he finally turned away from his inspection he found Alice quite herself again. She was listening to the store proprietor's version of the affair, a story that, under the stimulus of Alice's dark eyes, lost none in the telling, for where facts failed him, imagination did not.

"—flew open before my very eyes," he was saying when Ralph turned around, "as if by unseen hands. And then this terrible sound—I can't scarcely describe it, more like (his eye fell on the ultra-ray apparatus), more like a great machine than anything else. I says to myself, says I, 'There's something strange about this,' I says, 'I'd better be on the lookout, I might be needed, for it looks to me,' I says, 'as though someone was up to something'."

As a matter of fact, he had thought the opening of the door due to a passing wind, and the hissing of the machine, which has already been likened to the buzz of an insect, the humming of a bee, let in by the same agency.

"And then that black man, he gave me a fright for fair," he went on.

"What about him? What was he like?" asked Ralph sharply.

"Ah," said the proprietor, swelling with importance, "that's just what I've been asking myself. Strange we should hit on the same thoughts ain't it?"

"Very," commented the scientist, with wasted irony. "Can't you give any description of him? When and how did you see him, anyway?"

The proprietor put his hands into his pockets and swayed backward and forward on the balls of his feet. He surveyed each member of his little audience with glances of poignant meaning, as one who had much of consequence to tell—all in good time.

Finally he spoke. "He was black," he said, "black all over."

"Yes, yes," exclaimed Ralph impatiently, "you told us that before. Can't you give us something definite to go by? His face, for instance. What was that like?"

The other leaned forward and tapped him on the chest impressively.

"Ay, that was black too," he said.

"Black!" cried Ralph.

"Black it was—all covered with a black cloth," said the none-too-intelligent shopkeeper smugly. "He come right out of the air before my very eyes, all black, with a black cloth on his face, and rolled out of my store like a cyclone."

"You should have tried to hold him," said Ralph.

"Well, I gave him a look, I can tell you. He won't forget it in a hurry. I just stood there and looked at him—like this."

He screwed up his face in so alarming a manner that one of Ralph's assistants was moved to remark that it was a wonder he didn't drop dead with a face like that.

"What d'ye mean?" demanded the owner of the countenance in question.

"I said," repeated the assistant, "it was a wonder he didn't drop dead. I would have. It's all I can do to look at you right now."

Alice, unable to control her laughter any longer, hastily murmured something about "fresh air" and went to the door.

Ralph, keeping his own face straight by a valiant effort, ordered his men to lift the ultra-ray machine and take it back to the laboratory to give it a more minute inspection at his leisure.

The girl and the man were very silent on their way back to Ralph's home. A tragedy had been narrowly averted and each felt that this first attempt might by no means be the last.

Only once did Alice voice her fears.

"You know," she said, "I am certain it was Fernand." She hesitated for a brief moment and then held out her hand. In the palm lay a small heart-shaped object of a curious translucent green, delicately carved. It was pierced for a chain, and indeed, a part of the chain still hung there, but it had been broken off short, and only a few links remained.

"What's that?" asked Ralph.

"A charm that Fernand always carries. He showed it to me once. He's very superstitious about it, he told me— and I found it back there in the store when I went to the door."

Ralph looked very thoughtful.

"Then he must have brought that machine from Mars," he said with decision. "And with such resources at his command, I wonder what his next move will be."

9

THE CONQUEST OF GRAVITATION

ALICE and her father had been invited, the next day, to Ralph's laboratory, as he wished to show them some of his latest discoveries. They found him sitting in front of his desk while he was engaged in dictating scientific data to thin air.

"Ah!" said Alice, as she entered, "you are evidently using some of the methods of my kidnapper, since you seem to be dictating to an invisible secretary!"

"Nothing so complicated," said Ralph.

Ralph, who then welcomed them, denied the charge, and went on to explain to his party his new invention.

"The evolution of letter-writing has been a slow and painful one. Our remote ancestors, many thousands of years ago, carved their letters in stone slabs. Later on, the more civilized Egyptians wrote their letters upon papyrus. Still later, upon the invention of paper and ink, communications and letters could be written much better and faster in that improved manner. Later still, the typewriter came into use.

"All of these methods had one great drawback. It was possible to easily falsify such records. While there had been handwriting experts, it happened very frequently in olden times—too frequently, in fact—that a signature on such an important document as, for instance, a will, was forged, and it became a question for handwriting experts to decide whether the signature was genuine. But even the handwriting experts were not always right.

"It has often occurred to me that it should be possible to use the human voice as it own document so that it could be preserved in a different manner than the phonographic method discovered in the 20th century. Of course, under that method it was possible for one to speak one's last will and testament, but it was a clumsy way and was rarely used on account of its high cost. Furthermore it was difficult to make copies of a talk. Then, too, the dise or cylinder upon which the phonographic records were made were very fragile, and could be broken, either accidentally or purposely.

"The method you see me using is phonetic, and it is practically impossible to falsify such a record. Watch how the machine works."

Ralph reseated himself at his desk and started to talk. Facing him on the desk was a machine of about the shape of an old-fashioned typewriter, except that there were no keys. There were a few dials and knobs and from the top of the cabinet a white sheet of paper slowly emerged as Ralph dictated. When he had finished, he pressed a button and the entire sheet was ejected. It was covered with queer-looking wave lines, similar to the lines made by a seismograph when recording earthquakes—queer little parallel lines with humps at the tops that increased from very short wave-like scrolls to long ones. The entire sheet was covered with these lines in indelible ink. Ralph showed Alice the page and went on explaining:

"The page which you see here is an exact record of my voice, but just as no two fingerprints are alike in this world, no two voices are alike either. Each has certain characteristics produced by certain overtones in the voices of the various individuals. The pronunciation of individuals varies, so does the intonation, so does the speed of talking, so does the timbre of the voice, and a hundred other differences that to an expert are observable immediately.

"Suppose, then, during my life I have recorded a great many documents similar to this one. The waves traced on this piece of paper have certain characteristics, which are entirely individual. Here are two sheets of paper, both containing the Lord's Prayer, but spoken by two different individuals in my office. Both of these individuals have voices that are very nearly alike, yet, you can see how great a difference there is between the lines. On one sheet the lines are much heavier and swing in quite an apparently different manner.

"By reference to authentic documents of this character, it will be impossible to falsify any record by having some one else make such a spoken record. A will, or any other important document, will, in the future, be made by this machine and will do away with many court cases and much business squabble, and much shirking of responsibility.

"Furthermore, by my method it is possible with the same machine to make as many as twenty-five copies at one time, while the original is being made. This is done by a chemical process in the machine itself, the copies being simply thin chemical papers which are being developed at the same time as the voice-writing is being made.

"Reading these pages is not as difficult as you might think. It would be necessary, however, to know the *pho-*

nolphabet. The phonolphabet is not very much different from the alphabet that you now know. Every syllable and every consonant used by you makes a certain impression in my machine, and while it may vary, as explained before, still it remains roughly the same, exactly as handwriting by different persons may vary, but still you can read because the characteristics are the same. The same is true of my machine. By studying the characters of the phonolphabet, it is possible, within a few weeks, to learn how to read a phonetic letter, with the same ease that you read a handwritten or typewritten letter.

"I expect that in the schools of the future children will be taught the phonolphabet so that every one will be able to read phonetic records.

"Another feature of my invention is that if you do not wish to read the letter you can listen to it." Saying so, Ralph inserted the letter into an odd-shaped cabinet, which had a slot at the top. Two grippers slowly began to draw the paper into the inside of the machine. Ralph turned two knobs and pushed a button, and within a few seconds his own voice was heard with unmistakable clarity repeating what he had said fifteen minutes before.

"This machine, likewise, is very simple," said Ralph. "The ink tracing on the paper record is opaque, while the paper itself is more or less transparent under a strong light. A light-sensitive cell on the other side slowly moves from left to right, taking off the entire phonetic record, as it were. This light-sensitive cell moves in the same ratio and with the same speed that I originally dictated, and the words are reproduced exactly as I spoke them, by means of a loud-speaking telephone coupled to an amplifier.

"Thus it is now possible to have a double record; an audible and a written one, and with the two it is practically impossible to falsify records.

"As you know, there have been some big embezzlement scandals recently and it was not always possible to convict those suspected due to the clever methods which these swindlers used.

"One great advantage of the new system is that it is done entirely by machine and does away with the human element. I do not require my real secretary when I dictate. I sit alone in my study or office and simply talk."

"There is one unique place, I am sure you will be interested in." Ralph led the way to the elevator and they quickly shot up to the roof, where they boarded one of Ralph's flyers and with a few minutes were heading north. The machine rose until they were up about 20,000 feet. The cold made it necessary to turn on the heat in the enclosed cab. In the distance, just ahead there shortly appeared a brilliant spot of light suspended in the dark sky, which quickly increased in size as they approached. From a distance it appeared like an enormous hemisphere with the flat side facing the earth below. As they drew close, they could see that it was a great city suspended in the air apparently covered with a transparent substance, just as if a toy city had been built on a dinner plate and covered with a bell-shaped globe.

They alighted on the rim, at a landing stage outside the transparent covering. They were soon walking along a warm, beautifully laid out street. Here was neither bustle nor noise. The deepest calm prevailed. There were small houses of an old-fashioned design. There were shops in

131

great profusion. There were playgrounds, neatly-laid-out parks, but without looking at the humans that were walking around, the visitors felt as if they had gone back many centuries.

There were no power roller skates, no automatic vehicles. There were no aeroflyers beneath the glass ceiling. Instead a serene calm prevailed, while people with happy expressions on their faces were leisurely walking to and fro.

Very much puzzled, Alice wanted to know what this mysterious glass-encased city was.

"This," explained Ralph, "is one of our many vacation cities that I hope will soon dot every part of the world. People are living entirely too intensely nowadays and with the many functions that they have to perform, with all the labor-saving devices they have, their lives are speeded up to the breaking point. The businessman or executive must leave his work every month for a few days, if he is not to become a wreck. Heretofore we have sent him to the mountain tops or to the seashore; there he found no rest. The noise, even on top of the mountains, due to aeroflyers and other vehicles, did not give a man a real rest. On our floating city there is absolute rest. There is no noise, no excitement, not even a radio telephone.

"The city, 20,000 feet above the ground, is floating in perfectly clean and uncontaminated air. This air, while less dense than that further down, is renewed automatically every few hours. It is invigorating, just the same as mountain air with all its benefits.

"The roof is made of steel lattice work, thick glass panes being fitted in between the steel frames. The shape is in the form of a huge dome covering the entire city, which measures about a little over a mile in circumference. The height of the center of the dome from the floor of the city is about 200 feet. At night the city is illuminated by cold light from high frequency wires running below the dome, similar to the system now used to light up our cities.

"The floor upon which the entire city rests is steelonium, and the city is held up by means of anti-gravitational impulse. By neutralizing the gravity for the area below the floating city and a little beyond it, it is possible to keep the floating city at any distance from the earth. In other words, we use a gravitational 'screen,' and then build a city on top of this screen.

"By charging the gravitational screen at a very high potential, we nullify gravity and as the city no longer has any weight it can be placed on any level and remain there practically indefinitely. A few air propellers keep the city from being blown away by storms or wind.

"Although it was very cold in our aeroflyer as we came up, it is nice and warm on the streets here. Nor is there any artificial heating during the daytime. There is perpetual sunshine during the day at this level, at which practically no clouds ever form.

"The city being entirely roofed over by the glass dome, and the interior being filled with air, the sun quickly heats up the atmosphere. Within two hours after the sun rises the air is balmy, and it would become stifling hot if the air was not renewed from time to time. Air is a poor conductor of heat, and if the air were not renewed, it would soon be 150 degrees in the shade. Cold air, however, from the outside, is continually drawn in so that an even temperature is maintained. Only at night is the city heated artificially, as without the sunlight at this altitude it soon becomes exceedingly cold.

"All the heating is done by electricity, and a uniform temperature is maintained during the night, which is somewhat less than the temperature during the day.

"There is nothing that a man or woman can do up here except rest, and that is precisely what they do. One week's rest up here is equivalent to a month's rest down below."

Ralph, with Alice and her father strolled through the suspended city in which the simple life was the keynote. There were recreation parks, gymnasiums, baths of various kinds, such as hydrotherapy, electrotherapy, and others. There were sun parlors and sun baking parks. The din of the city, the curse of man's own handiwork, was absent. Everyone wore either felt or rubber shoes. The entire atmosphere was delightful and restful.

It was with genuine regret that Alice and her father returned to the aeroflyer and back to New York.

That night after dinner Ralph took his guests to a new entertainment that had just become popular. They entered a big building on which, in big fiery letters, was inscribed

GRAVITATIONAL CIRCUS

Ralph explained to his guests that with the invention of the nullifying of gravitation, many new and wonderful effects had come about. Gravity, he explained, was an electromagnetic manifestation, in the ether, the same as light, radio waves, etc. It had always been the dream of scientists for hundreds of years to nullify the effect of gravitation. "In other words," Ralph continued, "if you pick up a stone and open your hand, the stone will fall to the ground. Why does it fall? First, because the earth attracts the stone, and second because the stone attracts the earth. There is a definite gravitational pull between the two. The effect of the stone in pulling up the earth is, however, inconsequential, and while the stone does exert a certain amount of pull towards the earth, the latter is so tremendously larger that the effect on the earth is not felt at all.

" 'If,' scientists had argued for hundreds of years, 'you could interpose between the stone and the earth a screen which nullified gravitation, the stone would not fall down when let go, but would remain suspended just exactly where you left it.'

"Scientists also argued that if gravitation was an electromagnetic manifestation of the ether, it should be possible to overcome and nullify it by electrical means.

"It took hundreds of years, however, before the correct solution was found. It was known that certain high frequency currents would set up an interference with the gravitational waves, for it had been found in the first part of our century that gravitation was indeed a wave form, the same as light waves, or radio waves. When this interference between the two waves, namely, the gravitational waves and the electrical waves was discovered, it was found that a metallic screen charged by electric high frequency waves would indeed nullify gravitation to a certain extent. If you charged a metal netting in this fashion and you weighed yourself on a spring scale on top of the screen, insulated of course from the screen itself, your weight would be roughly diminished one-half.

"In other words, about half of the gravitation had been

nullified, the other half still remaining. Thus things stood until about two years ago, when I began to occupy myself with the problem. I reasoned that while we had achieved much, still much more remained to be done. Our anti-gravitational screen still let through some of the gravitational waves, or fifty percent of the energy, which we could not seem to counteract. I felt that it was not so much the effect of the current as the material of the screen which seemed to be at fault. Experimental work along this line convinced me that I was on the right track and that if ever gravitation was to be annulled in its entirety a screen of a special material would have to be evolved in order to obtain the desired results.

"I finally found that only the densest material known, namely thoro-iridium, would completely stop the gravitational waves, providing that the metal screen was uninterruptedly bombarded with alpha rays which are continually emitted by radium.

"The screen finally evolved was expensive to make at first, but quantity production now has very considerably lowered the price."

By this time the party had found their seats in the amphitheater, and they had seated themselves. Seats were all around a ring, which did not look much different from the old-fashioned circus ring, except that it was, perhaps, a little larger. The gravitational screen, Ralph explained, was located below and could not be actually seen. The machinery, too, was located in the basement. A fine wire netting surrounded the entire arena, from top to bottom, the purpose of which became apparent later.

It was an old-fashioned horse and bareback rider act. Suddenly the gravitation was cut off, and the horse rose, beating the air with his hoofs, while the rider, in a sitting position hung onto the horse with his legs. The horse and rider no longer having any weight, they could not of course entirely control their movements. Both horse and rider at times hung with their heads downwards, then sideways, until finally, by jerking, they arrived in the center of the arena.

The horse had been well trained and ceased pawing the air, and his legs hung limp.

The rider mounted on the back of the horse, and with a slight jump reached the ceiling of the arena, some hundred feet up. Having no weight left, he bounced by the least muscular effort. Pushing against the ceiling with one of his fingers, he bounded down to the floor of the arena, only to rebound again to the ceiling. He kept this up for a few minutes, and then repeated the same thing sideways, where he hit against the wire netting, stretched from top to bottom of the arena to keep the performer from falling into the audience.

The gravitational field extended only vertically, but was not in evidence immediately beyond the sides of the arena. Had there been no screen, the performer, when passing outside the gravitational boundary, would have immediately regained his full weight and would have fallen.

The performer could jerk himself around anywhere in the arena, and being a good acrobat, he had no difficulty in reaching his horse. Much care had to be exercised, however, because the slightest kick against the horse would have sent the horse to the opposite side.

Slowly the gravitation was turned on, and both horse and rider sank gracefully toward the ground, where with the full gravitation restored, the horse and rider made their exit.

The next act was one that even Ralph had not seen. Two experts at juggling bounded into the arena and after the gravitation was cut off one of them placed a billiard cue on his forehead, and an old-fashioned hand lamp on top of the cue. The juggler then took the cue away and withdrew jerkily. The lamp remained in the same position, until brought down by one of the performers.

The tricks aroused great enthusiasm among the audience. An acrobat, using one of the billiard cues as a standing trapeze, revolved around the trapeze as if it were held securely in place. By jerking around the billiard cue, it was made to appear as if he was actually swinging around under his full "weight."

A beautiful effect was obtained when the jugglers brought several colored glass pitchers, filled with different-colored liquids. When the pitchers were inverted, nothing happened, because the liquid, having no weight, could not flow out. However, by turning the pitcher upside down and suddenly jerking it away the colored liquid, due to its own lag or inertia, stayed behind.

Due to the surface tension of liquids, it did not retain the shape of the pitcher, but formed itself immediately into a globe. The jugglers emptied a number of pitchers all in a row, leaving behind the globular liquid balls, formed of water and fruit juices.

The jugglers approached the balls and began to drink, simply by placing their lips against them. They then demonstrated the mobility of the water balls by pushing their fingers into them and cutting the balls in two, the halves immediately becoming new and smaller balls.

Then by carefully giving each of the balls a slight push, the water balls would gravitate up to the ceiling of the arena and still having enough momentum left they would rebound and come back, only to be pushed up again by flat tennis racquets.

This had to be done carefully because the slightest false motion spread out the water balls into a flat sheet. The surface tension of the liquid always reasserted itself and the water balls came down sometimes in an elliptical shape. Every time the flat tennis racquet hit the balls, they lost their shape momentarily, but soon were globular again.

The two jugglers finally managed to push the liquid spheres one into another, until finally all balls had been joined into one. This, of course, amalgamated the various colors, but the colors had been made in such a way that the ball became a somewhat dirty-looking white, all the colors having recombined, making one color, just as all the hues of the rainbow, if combined together, make white.

The final act was where a huge water ball, about twenty-five feet in diameter, was pushed to the center of the arena, while a number of pretty girls entered the liquid itself and swam within the ball. The ball was lit up by strong searchlights, and the entire arena darkened, as the girls swam within the clear crystal water ball. When the swimmers needed air, all they had to do was to push their heads out of the sphere, breathe, and then resume "swimming," or jerking themselves around within the weightless water.

10

TWO LETTERS

DURING SEPTEMBER Alice and her father had remained Ralph's guests, extending their stay at his urgent request. James 212B 422 made a most satisfactory chaperon. If they visited one of the great historical museums he always managed to disappear in search of some exhibit, leaving the other two to sit on a bench to wait his return, which was often delayed purposely.

But to his daughter and the scientist time had become of little importance and though the engineer was sometimes gone an hour, when he returned he would find them still sitting on the bench, sometimes deep in conversation, sometimes absorbed in a silence that meant more than any words could express.

Together they were blissfully happy, apart they were wretchedly lonely.

Ralph, it appeared, had completely forgotten numerous of his lectures in which he had labeled love as "nothing but a perfumed animal instinct." No lover more abject than he now, none more humble in the presence of his divinity. During those weeks they had arrived at a mutual understanding.

All the world knew and rejoiced in their happiness. Ralph had always been extremely popular with the people. Even the Planet Governor himself had been moved to privately express his approval. Many times had the scientist worried him. Ralph had so often been restive under the restraints which must of necessity be imposed upon one so important to the Earth's progress. And now, with this new influence to hold him, the Governor felt that the task of keeping Ralph contented had been lifted from the official's already over-burdened shoulders.

All the world rejoiced—all but two, and for them the knowledge of the two lovers' happiness was gall and wormwood.

One was roused to fury, the other plunged in despair.

To Fernand the scientist was one hitherto unforeseen obstacle to be removed from his path in his conquest of Alice. To the Martian, knowing beforehand that his passion was hopeless, the knowledge that she loved another was, nevertheless, a bitter blow. Before, at least, she had been heartfree. Wretched as he had been, bitter as he had been against the laws that made such a union impossible, there had been the barren comfort of the fact that she belonged to no one else. Now, even that was taken from him, and he felt that he could bear no more.

In his desperation he made up his mind to leave Earth, and immediately booked his passage to Mars. But on the very eve of his departure he found himself unable to make the decision that would separate him from her forever, and the next inter-planetary liner, which left Earth for Mars, carried, not himself, but this code letter to his best friend on his distant planet.

To Rrananolh AK 42,   New York, September 20, 2660.

Although I am booked on the *Terrestrial* which departs tomorrow, I have cancelled my reservation and consequently will not arrive on Mars November 31st as planned. I do not know whether I shall take passage on the next transport or not. In fact, I don't know what I shall do. I am mad with despair and anguish. A thousand times over have I wished that I had never come to this planet!

I have not told you before, but as perhaps you have guessed from my previous letters, I am in love with a Terrestrial woman. Never mind her name. I loved her from the first moment I saw her. You, who have never visited the Earth, can hardly understand. It does not matter.

I have tried in every way to free myself from this mad infatuation, but it is hopeless. Chemicals and Radio-treatments seem but to accentuate my longing for that which is forever beyond my reach. I thought at first that I could conquer myself, but I know now that I cannot, and the knowledge is driving me to madness.

She has never known, and I think no one else here does. I have told none but you, my friend. Always I feared that in some way I might betray myself to her. There are times now when I wish that I had.

And yet—to have her suffer as I am suffering—I could not have borne that.

I will, I suppose, go the way of all Martians who have had the misfortune to care for a Terrestrial. A little *Listadinide* injected under the skin will free me from an existence which has become a daily torture unless I find a way to evade the harsh laws.

Please hand the enclosed documents to my Second. If I do not see you again do not grieve for me, but remember our friendship, and think sometimes of your unhappy friend.
LLYSANORH'

Long after his missive had gone, he sat rigid, motionless, by the window with unseeing eyes fixed on the city below him. At last he rose with a sigh and left the room. Was there no way out of such misery? Was there no straw he could grasp?

Of a very different caliber was an epistle sent by Fernand 60O 10 to his friend Paul 9B 1261.

New York, Sept. 28th, 2660.

Dear Paul:

You have heard the gossip, but don't fear my having a broken heart. I am not easily downed, and I have a card or two yet to play in this game.

Fact is, Alice is as hard to conquer as a steelonium wall is to break through. That, however, is to my liking, my dear Paul. I love obstacles, particularly when the goal is as pretty as Alice. I have never wanted her more than now that she has thrown me down. Perhaps if she had ever encouraged me I would not have cared a rap for her. But—this opposition inflames me! Now I will have her. I *will* have her, and she shall love me, mark my words.

I have mentioned to you before the ridiculous Martian, Llysanorh', I believe. It is very amusing to see him staring at Alice with adoration in those enormous eyes of his. I really believe he is in love with her, but these Martians are so self-controlled it is hard to tell anything about them.

If Alice had fallen in love with this lanky, seven-foot Llysanorh' she would have been lost to me, and to all the rest of the world. That fellow certainly can be sugary when he wants to. However, she really imagines that she's in love with this crazy scientist, and right now I'm de-

143

cidedly *de trop*. That worries me very little, I assure you. She will soon learn to love me once I can get her away from him. And I am going to provide for that.

Everything has been arranged, and I am only awaiting my opportunity. If I am successful, I will take her out into space for a few months. My machine is in readiness. It is the latest type, and the finest I have ever seen. Provisions, books, reels for the Hypnobioscope, instruments, etc., in fact, everything you can think of is on board. I have even provided a well trained maid. I can assure you Alice won't find it lonesome. Besides, I flatter myself that I can be very entertaining.

Before I close I must ask you to attend to several matters for me, as per enclosed rolls. You will understand everything better after you read the instructions. I do not expect to be away more than three months at the latest, and you will see from the gray document that I empower you to take charge of my affairs. I will send you a message from on board the machine if all goes well.

Until then,

Fernand.

It was the night of the full moon. There was a faint touch of crispness in the early autumn breeze that now and again gently ruffled the waters of the ocean. A thousand stars danced lightly in the sky and were reflected in the undulating waves below. And in the moonlit path over the waters hovered an aerocab gleaming silvery white in the radiance.

The cab was far from New York, away from the beaten traffic. Occasionally other aircraft came into view but always at a distance.

To Alice and Ralph this solitude was Paradise. Night after night they hired an aerocab and flew to this lonely airway, where seated side by side, with only the driver for a chaperon, they were absolutely happy.

The driver was a silent man who, as long as he was well paid for his time, was content to describe endless circles indefinitely.

On this particular evening Alice seemed, to Ralph, more lovely than he had ever before seen her. In the caressing light of the mellow moon her flowerlike face glowed with a new radiance, and her dark eyes, shadowed with long curling lashes, were mistily tender.

Between these two there was no need for words. So perfectly were their thoughts attuned that each knew what the other felt.

And so, presently, their hands stole out and met, and clasped. And it seemed to both that Heaven could hold no greater happiness than this, until, with one accord, they turned their faces to each other, and their lips met. To them nothing existed beyond themselves and their love.

The voice of another aerocab driver hailing them made them realize that there were still ties that bound them to Earth, and they moved apart a little self-consciously, as a cab drew alongside their own.

"Having some trouble with my motor," called the newcomer. "Could you let me have a few copper connectors to repair the damage?"

"Sure," returned their driver, and the two cabs came together and were made fast.

Ralph, seeing that his man could attend to the matter, turned away from them towards Alice, and again drew her hand into his own, where it snuggled confidingly.

Quite suddenly he was aware of a sickish, sweet odor, which almost instantly became suffocating. He was conscious of the pressure of Alice's fingers and then blackness overwhelmed him.

11

THE FLIGHT INTO SPACE

How LONG he was unconscious Ralph did not know, but when he came to his senses the moon had sunk low on the horizon. He felt unbearably weary and his limbs seemed too heavy to move. For a time he half lay in his seat looking stupidly down at the ocean, his mind a blank.

All at once it dawned upon him that the seat next to him was empty. "Alice, Alice," he muttered, trying to shake off his stupor, "Alice, where are you?"

There was no reply. The driver, his hands on the steering disc, was slumped forward in his seat, his head sunk on his breast.

With a stupendous effort Ralph managed to open the glass window in front of him. Instantly the strong odor of chloroformal almost overpowered him, and a terrible sensation of nausea forced him to cling blindly to his seat. In a moment it passed and he was able to collect his senses somewhat. His first thought was for Alice. His dimmed sight had cleared sufficiently for him to see that she was not in the cab. He thought she must have fallen into the sea, and in his agony he cried aloud her name again and again.

And then a recollection came to him, of her father's words on the first morning of their visit. He had feared for Alice. Someone had threatened her. Ralph forced his still wandering mind to concentrate. Some one had threatened to kidnap her, and that someone was Fernand 600 10.

He recalled the stranded aerocab. Its helplessness had been a trick to deceive him, and to get near enough to drug him and his driver while they took Alice away.

The thought aroused him from his dreadful lethargy. With a rush his vitality came back. He flung himself upon the stupefied driver and shook him violently.

The cab was still flying at an even speed in a great circle and Ralph saw that it was imperative that he get control of it at once, for another machine, bound evidently for New York, was bearing down upon the helpless men.

With a powerful shove he got the driver into the auxiliary seat and climbed over, seizing, as he did so, the steering disc. He flung it over, just in time to escape the onrushing cab, whose occupants, as it passed, leaned out, and in fluent profanity inquired if he wanted the whole airway.

Unheeding, Ralph set the steering disc toward New York, and proceeded to lighten the cab. Overboard went the glass doors, cushions, matting, even the hood of the machine. Everything that he could wrench off he tossed to the dark waters beneath him.

The cab, relieved of the weight of its equipment shot ahead at tremendous speed, and in less than ten minutes dropped onto the landing place on top of the scientist's laboratory. Leaving the driver where he was Ralph dashed into the building. Meeting Peter he did not stop, only motioned him to the cab while he himself sprang to the nearest Telephot. And within fifteen minutes every detective and special agent had been notified of the disappearance of Alice. Ralph had immediately transmitted the lost girl's photograph to the Central Office where it was placed before a Telephot connecting with every member of the entire police force, and the picture was reproduced for them in their portable radio instruments for ten seconds, enabling them to get her features firmly impressed on their minds.

His next act was to call the Intercontinental Hotel where Fernand had been stopping.

Upon inquiry he was informed that Fernand had left three hours ago with his baggage. His destination was unknown.

"I knew it!" Ralph muttered to himself.

On second thought it occurred to him that it might be of advantage to visit the hotel, and as it was only a few blocks away he flew over to it, leaving his assistants in charge of his radio stations, with strict orders to record every message, to tune into everything, and to take the messages down on the recorder discs.

At the hotel he was recognized at once, and as the news had spread over the city like wild-fire, he was treated with every consideration.

He closely questioned everyone and then asked to see the rooms which Fernand 600 10 had occupied.

The rooms were just as their occupant had left them and Ralph requested that he be undisturbed there for a short time.

He examined every nook and corner without finding anything to give him a clue to Fernand's whereabouts, and he was about to leave when his eye caught the reflection of a light-ray falling on a bright object under the dresser.

Insignificant as the little metal object was, it was enough to convey a fearful picture to his mind. He recognized it at once as a metal turning belonging to the balancer of the *Gyro-Gyrotor* of a *Space Flyer*. Evidently the metal part had been dropped and Fernand had not had the time to look for it. Ralph decided that Fernand had obtained a supply of the parts which are only required on a prolonged flight into space.

He was now positive that Fernand 600 10 had carried off his sweetheart in a space flyer and that the machine by this time was probably far away from the earth, headed for unknown regions. It would also be practically impossible to follow without knowing the direction of the space-defying machine.

In a daze Ralph returned to his laboratory, where he again called the Central Office. As all space flyers must be licensed by law, he had no trouble in getting the information he desired. A new machine of a well-known Detroit firm had been registered four days ago, and the description of the owner answered to that of Fernand 600 10.

Late as it was, Ralph immediately communicated with the Detroit manufacturer, who, upon hearing his reasons for the request, supplied him with all the necessary details.

Ralph learned from him that the purchaser of the new machine, one of the very latest models, was Fernand, beyond any doubt, and when he was informed that the latter had plentifully supplied himself with spare parts as if for a long journey, and moreover, the most significant fact that the cabin had been fitted out as a lady's boudoir, then indeed were his worst suspicions confirmed.

The manufacturer also told him that the entire outside shell was of *Magnelium*—an invention of Ralph's—and that this flyer was the first to be equipped with the new metal.

As he concluded his conversation and disconnected, Ralph brought his clenched fist down upon the desk. "Magnelium," he muttered between set teeth, "the only machine out in the universe made with Magnelium. Magnelium, my own Magnelium, about which no one in the world knows more than I do. Perhaps the odds are not all with you, Fernand, damn you!"

At first thought it might be considered a difficult feat accurately to locate a machine thousands of miles from the earth, speeding in an unknown direction somewhere in the boundless universe. The feat was easy to the scientist. As far back as the year 1800 astronomers accurately measured the distance between the earth and small celestial bodies, but it was not until the year 2659 that Ralph 124C 41 + succeeded in accurately determining the exact location of flyers, in space, beyond the reach of the most powerful telescope.

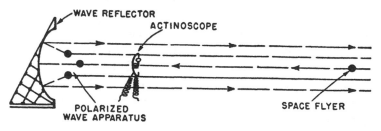

WAVE REFLECTOR
ACTINOSCOPE
POLARIZED
WAVE APPARATUS
SPACE FLYER

A *pulsating polarized ether wave,* if directed on a metal object can be reflected in the same manner as a light-ray is reflected from a bright surface or from a mirror. The reflection factor, however, varies with different metals. Thus the reflection factor from silver is 1,000 units, the reflection from iron 645, alomagnesium 460, etc. If, therefore, a polarized wave generator were directed toward space, the waves would take a direction as shown in the diagram, provided the parabolic wave reflector was used as shown. By manipulating the entire apparatus like a searchlight, waves would be sent over a large area. Sooner or later these waves would strike a space flyer. A small part of the waves would strike the metal body of the flyer, and these waves would be reflected back to the sending apparatus. Here they would fall on the *Actinoscope* (see diagram), which records only reflected waves, not direct ones.

From the actinoscope the reflection factor is then determined, which shows the kind of metal from which the reflection comes. From the intensity and the elapsed time of the reflected impulses, the distance between the earth and the flyer can then be accurately and quickly calculated.

The reflection factor of Magnelium being 1060, Ralph succeeded in locating Fernand's space flyer in less than five hours' search. He found that Fernand's machine at that time was about 400,000 miles distant from the earth and apparently headed in the direction of the planet Venus. A few seconds' calculation showed that he was flying at the rate of about 45,000 miles an hour. This was a great surprise to Ralph and it puzzled him somewhat. He knew that Fernand's machine was capable of making at least

75,000 miles an hour. Ralph reasoned that if he were in Fernand's place, he would speed up the flyer to the utmost.

Why was Fernand flying so leisurely? Did he think himself secure? Did he think that nobody could or would follow? Or was he having trouble with the *Anti-Gravitator*?

Ralph could not understand it. However, his mind had already been made up. He would pursue Fernand even though it took him into those parts of the solar system yet uncharted, and, if necessary—kill him!

It was now noon, and he gave sharp, quick instructions to his assistants, ordering his space flyer, the "Cassiopeia," to be made ready at once. Provisions sufficient to last for six months were put on board and Ralph himself installed a great number of scientific instruments, many of which he considered he might find useful. He also ordered a large number of duplicate parts of the flyer's machinery to be stowed on board in case of emergency.

To the astonishment and dismay of Peter and the others, the scientist announced his intention of making the journey alone.

"The fight is to be man against man, brain against brain," he said as he stood by his space flyer which was in readiness upon the tower-platform. "Today it is not brute force that counts, but scientific knowledge. I will demonstrate to the world that crimes of this kind need not be tolerated."

He stepped onto the running board as he spoke and was about to step into the flyer when the sound of an aeroflyer descending close by made him hesitate. It was a government flyer, and even as Ralph paused, it landed on the platform beside his own machine, and a smartly uniformed young official sprang from the seat beside the driver. Saluting Ralph he handed him a transcribed telegram with the words:

"Message from the Planet Governor, sir."

Dismay seized the scientist, as, breaking the seal of the wrapper, he read the printed words:

> Unipopulis, Sept. 34, 2660,
> Planet Governor's Capitol.

I have just received news of the calamity that has befallen you.

I extend to you my sincere sympathy.

I will this afternoon place at your disposal six Government space flyers, the crews of which are absolutely under your instructions.

I must, however, caution you not to enter into any pursuit in person.

As Planet Governor it is my duty to advise you that you have not the right to place your person in unnecessary danger.

Allow me furthermore to point out to you that under the law "+" scientists are not allowed to endanger their lives under any circumstances.

I therefore command you not to leave the earth without my permission.

I have ordered your space flyer to be guarded.

> In high esteem,
> William Kendrick 21K 4,
> *The 18th Planet Governor.*

To
Ralph 124C 41 +,
New York.

Ralph read the radiogram twice before he folded it slowly and deliberately thrust it into his pocket.

Then slowly withdrawing his hand and extending it to the government official, he said:

"Well, I must obey orders."

The official took the proffered hand, and no sooner had he grasped it than he stiffened and became as rigid as stone.

With one bound Ralph was in his machine crying to the stupefied audience:

"Don't worry about him. I pricked his hand with a little *Catalepsol*. In fifteen minutes he will be all right again."

He slammed the door of his space flyer and simultaneously the machine rose as if shot from a cannon, and in ten seconds was lost to sight.

Since the Dark Ages, men have had a powerful longing to leave Earth and visit other planets. Towards the end of the twenty-first century, when atmospheric flying had become common, scientists began seriously to think of constructing machinery to enable man to leave the confines of the planet to which humanity had been chained for ages.

Towards the beginning of the twenty-second century economic conditions had become acute and the enormous population of Earth, which had passed the twelve billion mark, clamored for an adequate outlet which the planet itself could no longer furnish.

The moon was regarded with longing eyes, and although that body was known to have no atmosphere and was known to be sterile, it was equally well known that Earth's scientists and engineers felt that they could, in a few years' time, make it habitable.

Atmospheric flying machines were, of course, totally unsuited, as they could not even reach the limits of the Earth's atmosphere, only forty miles away.

Obviously to reach the moon or any other celestial body, it was necessary to devise a method of overcoming the enigmatical force known as the Earth's gravity, which chains all bodies to the planet.

A multitude of inventions and suggestions were made, but none proved to be of any value until the *Anti-Gravitator* was invented by the American 969L 9 in the year 2210.

This scientist had made extensive studies of the gyroscope and had finally evolved a machine which when set in motion would rise freely and continue to rise as long as power was supplied.

The action, moreover, was purely gyroscopic.

969L 9 took a large hollow sphere (the rotor) inside of which he built a number of independent gyroscopes, all of which traveled in fixed orbits. The large sphere which hung in a gyroscopic frame was made to spin around on its axis at great speed. This sphere thus acted as the flywheel of a gyroscope and as such was not influenced by the so-called *horizontal gravity*. As in the case of simple gyroscopes, its axis would always be in a vertical line as long as the spheric rotor was in motion.

If, however, the independent gyroscopes inside of the sphere were set in motion by means of electrical current, the *Vertical Gravity* (weight) was overcome, the entire contrivance rising into the air, its rising (lifting) speed being directly proportional to the speed of the enclosed gyroscope rotors.

From 969L 9's experimental work the anti-gravitators were perfected, and it became possible to lift a weight of 1,000 kilograms with an anti-gravitator weighing but 12 kilograms.

Space flyers were equipped with from six to twelve large anti-gravitators attached to various points of their shells, all of which could be worked in unison, or operated independently in order to control the direction of the flyer.

As Ralph's space flyer rushed through the atmosphere, the friction of the machine against the air made the interior uncomfortably hot in spite of the fact that the machine had triple walls, the spaces between being filled with poor heat conducting materials.

After the flyer, however, had left the atmosphere, the stellar cold rapidly made itself felt.

Ralph then took his bearings, after he had verified, by means of the polarized wave transmitter that Fernand's flyer was still headed towards Venus. He then locked the steering disc and the space flyer continued its journey in a straight line of pursuit toward the machine of Fernand.

This done, Ralph flashed a radiogram asking the Planet Governor's indulgence for disobeying the law. Then he took his first look at the earth, which, since he was traveling at the rate of 80,000 miles an hour, had shrunk to the dimensions of a medium-sized orange. As he was flying toward the sun, Earth, being directly behind him was fully illuminated and appeared like a full moon. The continents and oceans were visible except where temporarily obscured by mist or clouds.

The general aspect of the Earth as seen from Ralph's flyer was that of a delicate faint blue green ball with white caps at each of the poles. The ball was surrounded by a pinkish ring near the circumference. This was the earth's atmosphere, the white caps being snow and ice around the north and south poles.

The brilliantly lighted earth was silhouetted against the inky black sky in sharp contrast.* The moon, hidden behind the earth, was not in evidence, when Ralph first looked earthward.

The stars shone with a brilliancy never seen from Earth; distant constellations which ordinarily cannot be seen, except, with a telescope, were plainly visible to him, in outer space.

The sun shone with a dazzling brilliancy in a pitch-black sky, and had he looked directly into its rays he would have been stricken blind.

The heat of the sun in the outside space when striking objects was tremendous. Had he held his hand against the glass window of the space flyer where the sun could strike it full, his hand would have been burned in a few seconds.

There was of course no night in the outer space (within the bounds of the planetary system). The sun shone uninterruptedly.

Time was an unknown quantity. Had it not been for the chronometer, reeling off seconds and minutes according to man's standard, time would cease to exist in a space flyer.

To a man who had never left the Earth, the phenomena

* In the outer space the "sky" is dead black; the blue color of the sky as seen from the earth is due to the atmosphere. The real sky is colorless.

encountered inside of a space flyer in the outer space was still more amazing.

"Weight" is synonymous with the gravity of the Earth. The denser a celestial body, the greater its gravity. The larger such a body is, the more strongly it will attract its objects. The smaller the body (if it has the same density), the smaller its force of attraction.

Thus a man weighing eighty kilograms on a *spring* scale on the earth, would weigh but thirty kilograms on the planet Mars. On the sun, however, he would weigh 2232 kilograms.

Inside of a space flyer, which had an infinitely small gravity, objects weighed practically nothing. They were heaviest near the walls of the machine, but in the exact center of the flyer, *all objects lost their weight entirely.* Thus any object, regardless of its earthly weight, *hung freely suspended in the center of the space flyer.* It could not move up or down, of its own accord, but hung stationary, motionless, like a balloon in the air.*

The occupant of a space flyer, having no weight, moved around with astonishing ease. He almost floated around in the machine. There was no physical labor. The biggest table was no heavier than a match. The passenger in a flyer could perform an incredible amount of work without tiring and without effort.

He could walk up the walls or walk "upside down" on the ceiling without danger of falling, as there is no "up" or "down" in outer space.

Sleep was practically impossible. There being nothing

* If a shaft were sunk to the center of the earth, an object placed there would stay suspended in space.

to tire the occupant, *sleep is unnecessary.* Dozing off is all he can do, and that could never last long, except after strenuous mental work.

As long as a space flyer was not too far distant from the sun (within the orbit of Mars, at least), little artificial heat was needed. The sun heated one-half of the flyer's shell to a fierce heat, but the side turned away from the sun was exposed to the terrible stellar cold (absolute zero) and a fairly comfortable temperature was the result.

The air supply was manufactured by chemical means on board, but very little was needed, as the original supply taken from the earth is used over and over by altering the carbonic acid gas by means of automatic generators.

It was of course of the utmost importance that no porthole or doors leading to the outside be opened. The air would have rushed from the flyer instantly, resulting in a perfect vacuum inside of the flyer, and instant death to all living organisms.

As the flyer moved away from a celestial body, the less the mechanical energy needed to propel it. There were of course exceptions. Thus between every two celestial bodies a point will be found where the attraction that one body exerts on the other is zero. If the flyer were brought to this point its gyroscopes could be at rest, as the machine would not be attracted by either body. It would "hang" between the two just as an iron ball hangs between two powerful magnets if carefully balanced. Give it the slightest push, however, and the ball will fly to either of the magnets.

The same was true of a space flyer, between two bodies at the "zero point." If it moved over that point it was immediately attracted by one of the bodies, and if its gyroscopes refused to work, the flyer would have been dashed to pieces against the attracting body.

If, however, the machine came to rest at the "zero point" it would begin to turn around on its own axis, while at the same time moving in an elliptical orbit around the sun—*the space flyer would become a tiny planet,* and as such was subject to the universal laws of the planetary system.

It was not hard to steer the space flyer; the nearer it came to a celestial body, the faster the gyroscopes worked; the further it drew away, the slower their movement.

After Ralph had thoroughly inspected the entire flyer he devoted his full attention to the course of Fernand's machine. At the rate at which he was flying he computed that he would overtake Fernand in ten hours, provided the latter did not increase his speed meanwhile.

Fernand, when Ralph left Earth, had a handicap of 400,000 miles. He was moving at the rate of 45,000 miles an hour. Ralph's machine had made 80,000 miles an hour since its start. If everything went well he would overtake the other in ten or eleven hours.

As there was nothing else to do, he busied himself in the laboratory near the conning tower at the top of the flyer in an attempt to make the hours pass more rapidly. With all its speed his machine seemed to crawl. He was in an agony of impatience.

At the end of the ninth hour he finally sighted Fernand's machine through his telescope. He then tried to signal Fernand by radio, but the other either did not hear or else did not want to answer.

Eleven hours after his departure from Earth, his machine drew to within a few hundred meters of Fernand's. After careful maneuvering he brought the machine parallel to the other, and looking through one of the heavy plate windows saw the strained, drawn and ghastly white face of Fernand staring at him.

Ralph moved a few levers and then closed a switch. A hissing sound was heard, and Fernand was seen to fall backwards, the window turning green at the same moment.

Ralph had struck him senseless with his *Radioperforer*.

In a few minutes he anchored his flyer to the other by means of a powerful electromagnet. He then pushed the connecting tube of his flyer into the tube-joint of Fernand's machine. With great care he made the joint airtight. Taking a coil of rope he opened the porthole and crawled through the tube leading into the other flyer.

Arrived at the other end he made sure that the joint at Fernand's machine was tight before he moved on.

Fernand lay unconscious on the floor and in a twinkling Ralph had bound him with the rope.

In high excitement he bounded upstairs to gain the room Alice should be occupying. His heart throbbed tempestuously. In another moment he would hold his sweetheart in his arms.

Arriving on the next floor he stood still for a moment and listened. There was no sound except for the gentle purring of the gyroscopic machinery.

He went from one room to another, then to the last one. The door was open. He entered with a strange feeling of dread. The room was empty. Apparently it had never been used.

In terror Ralph ran from one end of the flyer to the other. He looked in every corner, in every closet. He could find neither Alice nor her maid. Where were they hidden? To make sure he went all over the ground again more thoroughly.

After the most careful scrutiny of every inch of the machine he fell limply into a chair, and buried his face in his hands.

Alice was not on board the flyer!!

12

LLYSANORH' STRIKES

For some minutes, Ralph stood motionless, completely
bewildered. To have spent so much time and effort to no
avail, hours—days wasted in a fruitless search! The
thought was maddening.

Obviously, she was not on board Fernand's space flyer.
Where, then, was she? Certainly Fernand himself had
had no opportunity to hide her, unless his whole flight
into space were a trick to deceive the searchers, and that
was more than unlikely. Fernand was cunning—was this
some new piece of duplicity?

Turning from the empty room he ran down to where
Fernand lay, still unconscious. Kneeling by his side Ralph
applied a small electrical shocking device to the spine of
the insensible man, with the result that in a few minutes Fernand opened his eyes and stared dazedly into those
of his captor.

"Where is she?" asked Ralph hoarsely. "What have you
done with her? Answer me, or by God, I'll blow you into
Eternity!" and, aiming his Radioperforer at Fernand's
head, he spoke with such ferocity that the other shrank
involuntarily.

"I don't know," he muttered, weakly. "It's God's truth
I don't know. The Martian got her. He took her away

and left me drugged." His voice trailed off and he seemed about to collapse.

"You're a liar!" growled Ralph, but his tone lacked the conviction of the words. There was that in the other's voice that rang true. Mechanically, he cut the cords that bound Fernand, and the man rolled over helplessly. He was weak and dazed, and altogether too broken in spirit to make any further trouble. His nerve was gone.

Ralph propped him up against the wall, but he slumped over on his side limply. Impatient at the delay, Ralph went in search of water, and finding a pitcher of it in Fernand's laboratory, unceremoniously dumped the contents over the prone man's head. This had the desired effect of restoring him somewhat, and in a short time he was able to tell the story in detail.

"When I applied the chloroformal to you that night, I used the same drug on Alice, while Paul 9B 1261, a friend of mine, took care of your driver. We dragged Alice into our cab, and made for the outskirts of New York where I had the space flyer in readiness. A maid for her was already on board. We got Alice on and I put her in the care of Lylette, and in a few seconds we were off.

"When we got well out in space I locked the steering disc and helped the maid revive Alice, and in a few minutes she was herself again, which she fully demonstrated by slapping my face and then trying to tear me apart like a wildcat, when she found where she was." He gave a wry smile at the recollection.

"Go on!" snapped Ralph.

"It was an hour later, and we were burning up space, traveling at a rate of 70,000 miles an hour, that the radio signalling apparatus began ringing furiously. I tuned in, and heard a faint, gasping voice from somewhere out in the great void. With difficulty I learned that there was another space flyer somewhere near me, with two men and four women on board, and that their oxygen supply was being rapidly exhausted, due to the spoiling of some of the oxygen-producing chemicals. They asked for a small supply of oxygen, enough to get them back to Earth. Otherwise they would be doomed.

"Knowing myself to be safe from pursuit for some hours, even had you known I abducted Alice, I decided to aid the crippled flyer, and answered that I would assist them as soon as possible. I went up to the conning tower and, with the telescope, located the other machine. Then I reversed the anti-gravitator machinery and within a short time I had drawn up level with the flyer.

"We made fast, and ran the connecting tube between the two machines. When the joints were made air-tight I crawled through, and just as my head came through the opening into the other, two hands gripped me around the throat and I was jerked into the machine. I made a desperate effort to wrench myself free but I was absolutely helpless in such hands. I found myself gripped by Llysanorh', the Martian, and I might as well have fought a tiger as that seven-footer.

"He said nothing, only stared at me with his enormous eyes, while he dragged me to a small compartment, manacled my hands, and left me, locking the door behind him. But he was back in fifteen minutes or so, with a triumphant look in his eyes. He picked me up and pushed me through the connecting tube into my own flyer. He dragged me into my machine-room, and forced me to watch while he, using a big hammer, smashed the mechanism of my six anti-gravitators, so that I would not be able to steer, and could fly in only one direction. He ruined all the spare parts, to make sure that I could not make any repairs or replacements.

"Then catching me by the back of the neck, he said:

"'I intercepted your letter to Paul 9B 1261, and followed you. You didn't count on *me*, Fernand, when you stole Alice. Neither you nor that fool scientist Ralph 124C 41 + shall have her. *No* man shall have her but myself. I will kill her first. I don't know why I don't kill you, except that you are scarcely worth the trouble. You can't pursue me with your machine in this condition, and when—*if ever*—you are found, it will be too late.'

"'Good God, man,' I said, 'surely you won't take a helpless Terrestrial girl!'

"'It is only what you did,' he replied, 'and at least, I love her!' And with that he pressed a cloth saturated with some drug unknown to me against my face, and that is all I remember.

"I must have been unconscious at least six or seven hours and when I came to, it was another hour before I shook off the effects sufficiently to recollect anything. Llysanorh' had taken off the manacles, but I was as helpless as if I had been bound. I must have dozed off, for I had only just awakened when I looked out and saw your flyer approaching. And that's the whole story."

Ralph had listened to the amazing narrative with growing apprehension. He knew enough of the Martian character to realize that Alice was in the hands of a man who, once the die was cast, would stop at nothing. He had been hopelessly, pitifully in love with Alice. It was easy to see that, having, probably quite by accident, intercepted Fernand's letter to Paul telling of his plans, he had in a moment of desperation, born of despair, determined to carry her off himself. Perhaps, in the first place, he had only intended to save her from Fernand, and then, considering the small possibility of discovery and pursuit, had succumbed to his overwhelming passion for her, and abducted her instead of returning with her to Earth. But whither was he bound? Surely, not to Venus where the inhabitants were nearly all Terrestrials, and whose laws were identical with those of Earth.

Mars? Possible, but improbable, although Llysanorh' might have some friend in his sect who would perform the Martian marriage ceremony secretly. But even if this were the case where could he take his captive bride? They would not be permitted to live on Mars, neither would Earth or Venus accept them.

The intolerably hot planet Mercury was out of the question, and the two moons belonging to Mars had no atmosphere.

There remained only the Asteroids.

At this thought Ralph sprang to his feet with an exclamation.

"I've been a fool not to think of them before," he cried. "Of course he would get her to one of them, and once there she will be lost forever. Good God, I must find his machine and head him off before it's too late."

He turned savagely on Fernand still crouched against the wall. "I'm tempted to leave you to the fate the Martian intended for you. God knows it wouldn't be half what you deserve."

"Don't do that, in Heaven's name," mumbled the other. "Don't leave me here like this."

The scientist looked at him contemptuously for a moment.

"Bah!" he said scornfully, "can't you even take your medicine like a man? But I'll turn your machine around and direct it Earthward. You will intercept the Earth in about thirty hours. You can't steer, but you can accelerate or retard the speed of your flyer, and need not collide with the Earth if you are careful.

"And remember this," he added grimly, "if you and I ever meet again I will pound your miserable cowardly body into jelly!"

He turned his back on the abject man, and returned to his own flyer. Then he turned Fernand's machine around, disconnected the two from each other, and in a few seconds Fernand's flyer had disappeared.

Ralph sprang into action. He immediately began taking observations. These told him that it would take him at least thirty days to reach Mars, even though he forced his machine to the utmost. He could not travel over 90,000 miles an hour, but, on the other hand, he felt sure that Llysanorh's machine was incapable of making more than 85,000 miles an hour. But the Martian had a handicap of probably 600,000 miles, and if Ralph gained on him at the rate of only 5,000 miles an hour, it would take 120 hours, or five terrestrial days to overtake him.

Ralph turned his machine towards the point in space where Mars would be at the end of thirty days, and now set himself to the task of making a search for the other flyer with the polarized wave apparatus.

For four wearisome and anxious hours he sought through space perseveringly, and was at last rewarded by locating another machine which he was certain was that of the Martian, as he had reasoned, heading for Mars.

At the same time the results of his calculations dismayed him greatly, for they revealed that Llysanorh's machine was making no less than 88,000 miles an hour. At this rate, Ralph was gaining only 2,000 miles an hour, and it would take thirteen or fourteen days to overhaul the other flyer. But as the Martian could not hope to reach Mars under twenty-nine days himself, Ralph figured that he, barring some unforeseen accident, would overtake him long before he landed there.

It was absolutely imperative that he do so, for once the Martian left Mars and headed for the Asteroids further pursuit would be useless. There were over 4,000 of these little planets already known * and it would be the work of a lifetime to search on each one for the fugitive and his victim. Speedy action on Ralph's part was urgent.

These little Asteroids, revolving in an orbit between Mars and Jupiter were practically uninhabited, although most of the larger ones had a good atmosphere, and a fair climate, considering their distance from the sun.

Some of them were only a few miles in diameter, and the largest measured but 485 miles. An electromobile, running at the slow rate of 60 miles an hour could circle such a tiny planet in 24 hours!

The larger planetoids had a superb vegetation, and as the gravity on these bodies was only a fraction of that on the Earth, the trees and shrubs were gigantic, while colossal fruits and vegetables grew in abundance. These plants helped to create a dense atmosphere, in spite of the small gravity, and life, on one of these little planets, was,

* Up to 1911 over 650 Asteroids had been discovered.

in many respects, far more comfortable and pleasant than on Earth or Mars.

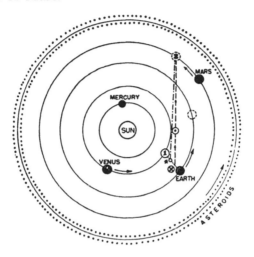

——— ORIGINAL DIRECTION OF RALPH
✹ WHERE RALPH OVERTOOK FERNAND
—·—·· NEW COURSE OF RALPH IN
     PURSUIT OF LLYSANORH'
② WHERE MARS WOULD BE AT END
   OF LLYSANORH'S JOURNEY

——— COURSE OF LLYSANORH'
⊙ POSITION OF LLYSANORH' WHEN
   RALPH OVERTOOK FERNAND
① WHERE VENUS WOULD HAVE BEEN MET
   IF FERNAND HAD CONTINUED HIS JOURNEY
⊗ WHERE LLYSANORH' ABDUCTED ALICE

Now began the hardest part of the chase for Ralph. There was nothing more to do than he had already done. From now on he must wait with what patience he could summon to his aid, until such time as his machine should catch up with that of the Martian. He could force his own no further, and he was very sure that Llysanorh' was also flying at his utmost speed.

At work, he had not had much time for thought.

Now, with time hanging heavily on his hands, his conjectures as to the fate of his sweetheart drove him, at times, nearly to madness.

13

ALICE OBJECTS

ALICE, on being aroused to consciousness by the ministrations of Lylette, the maid, and Fernand, and finding herself a prisoner on board a space flyer at the mercy of the latter, was overwhelmed with fury. This cool abduction of herself provoked her to such a passionate outburst that Fernand had actually retreated before it.

"You coward," she blazed, "how dare you keep me here! Turn around and take me back at once—at once, do you hear?"

Fernand, in the act of opening her door and going back to his laboratory, paused smilingly.

"My dear girl," he said mockingly, "ask of me anything and I will grant it—except that. You have a temper that delights me. Your smiles will be all the sweeter, later."

Her answer was to fly at him with such passion that he involuntarily took a step backwards. In a flash she had run by him, was down the stairs and tugging at the fastening of the door that led outward. Fernand bounded after her calling to Lylette as he ran, and in a moment they were both struggling with the girl, who had indeed become a veritable wildcat. She had both hands fastened around the great bar that held the door and fought madly to unfasten it. Let that door be opened the fraction of an inch and all three would instantly have been blown to pieces.

172

Fernand wrenched at her hands in real fear that she would succeed in her purpose, which was evidently their destruction.

She was a strong athletic girl, and at the moment her desperation gave her added vigor. But the combined strength, and by no means gentle handling of Fernand and Lylette, who herself was a large and powerfully built woman, forced Alice to relinquish her hold, and she was dragged, struggling, back to her room, and left there, with the door double-locked.

Alone, she passed from the high exaltation of anger to a state of nervous apprehension. Another woman in her place might have wept, have begged piteously for mercy where there was no mercy, but this girl was made of sterner stuff. She might be frightened but Fernand should never guess it.

Dry-eyed, with lips set in a firm line, lest they tremble and betray her, she sat facing the door, gripping in her small hands the only weapon she had been able to find— a small metal vase, having a round, and fairly thick base.

Knowing that Fernand would come back, prepared as she was for his return, she was unable to repress a start of genuine terror when she heard someone unbolting the door. She clutched the vase more tightly, white-faced, but courageous.

Fernand entered alone, carefully closing the door behind him. He wore his customary, rather bland smile, and his voice was suave to the point of oiliness.

"All over our little fit of temper?" he asked.

Alice stared at him, disdainfully, unanswering. Then her eyes fell upon something in his hand—manacles of glistening steelonium!

The horror she felt was depicted in her face, for he said, holding them out for her to see, "A pair of bracelets for you, sweetheart. Just as a precautionary measure. You are rather too quick with those hands of yours. But I am not unkind, my dear. You need not wear them if you will only give me your word not to repeat your recent performance."

Beyond the door she saw Lylette standing in readiness, and she knew that physical resistance would be ineffectual. Far better to give her promise and be free than to be bound and helpless. Besides, there was the laboratory. In it there were many roads to freedom—there were poisons that killed instantly and painlessly. Unmanacled she might reach them eventually. Bound, even that way would be closed.

Coldly, clearly, she gave her promise, but inwardly she offered up a prayer of thankfulness when he turned and handed the handcuffs to Lylette.

"You can lay down your weapon, Alice," he said, still with his mocking smile. "I can assure you that you have no need of it. You will find me a gentle lover, and one who is willing to wait for his lady's favors." He stopped suddenly, and turning his head in the direction of the stairs, listened intently.

From the laboratory, came the insistent ringing of the radio calling apparatus.

With a muttered order to Lylette, he was gone.

What was happening, Alice did not know. She could not read radio messages, but she knew that only something of grave import could have made Fernand rush like that to the radio. She strained her ears, but heard nothing.

Her hopes rose with a great bound with the thought

that perhaps Ralph was on his way to her. Perhaps it was he signalling. She had been sure that he would follow her as soon as possible, and now her dark eyes brightened with hope.

At this moment Lylette, without a glance in her direction, closed the door, and Alice was once more alone and a prisoner behind bolted doors.

It was then that she gave way to her loneliness and despair. She knew that if it had been Ralph signalling, Fernand would at once, having received the news that the scientist was in pursuit, set about making plans to elude him. She knew that Fernand was desperate, that his life, under the law, was forfeit for this crime he had committed. He would stop at nothing. Instinctively, she felt that he would destroy her and himself, rather than be taken. Certainly, he would not hesitate to murder Ralph if the opportunity presented itself.

She flung herself upon the couch, and burst into tears of agony, and terror. Suddenly she sprang to her feet, still sobbing, wide-eyed with dread of what she knew not.

The space flyer had stopped. The throb of the machinery had stilled and the flyer was hanging motionless in space.

Standing in the middle of the room, rigid with suspense, Alice waited with beating heart. Suddenly she heard the sound of rapid steps on the stairs. Now they halted at the door, and someone fumbled at the bolts and locks.

The next instant the door was flung wide open, and Llysanorh' the Martian stood upon the threshold!

14

THE TERROR OF THE COMET

DURING THE NEXT FEW DAYS Ralph passed midway between Earth and Venus. This was the spectacle that at times greatly increased the transport space flyer travel between Earth and Mars, many of the inhabitants of both planets making the long journey simply to get a view of the beautiful planet Venus.

Ralph ran almost parallel for a time with the two planets (see diagram), Venus to his left, Earth to his right. Although he was quite near the former he could hardly see it, as the bright rays of the sun precluded detailed observation. A few days later, however, it had swung sufficiently far enough to the left to afford him occasional glimpses of its beauties.

Ralph worked almost continuously in his laboratory in the conning tower. In the course of the week since he had left the Earth, he had only catnapped for about two hours, since sleep was impossible.

He constructed several new pieces of apparatus, which he considered might be useful in case of a possible encounter with Llysanorh'. He knew that Llysanorh' could not be as easily subdued or caught as Fernand. This tall Martian was an inventor himself and knew much about handling modern death-dealing weapons. It would be useless to try the Radioperforer as he probably would carry a Silonium armor, proof against all Radium emanations.

176

One of the first things he had done was to lead wires from the steering apparatus up to the conning tower. On the floor of the tower he arranged contacts in such a manner that he could press them together with his feet. The control was similar to the foot pedals of an organ. He then practised for some days until he could steer the flyer wholly with his feet. Thus his hands were free to control any apparatus he would need for attack or defense. With his feet he could so control the machine as to avoid projectiles if necessary.

As the days rolled by, however, Ralph became more and more disturbed. He now took observations hourly, his eyes glued to the indicator. With a sinking heart he saw that he was not gaining on the Martian. The latter had his machine well tuned up and was covering almost 90,000 miles an hour. At this rate Ralph could never catch up with Llysanorh'. It was maddening. The days became a long, drawn-out agony. Ralph had done everything in his power to accelerate the speed of his flyer and to strain the machinery further meant inviting certain death. Within eight days Llysanorh' would land on Mars —his course now plainly showed that he was headed for the planet. At best Ralph would be ten hours behind— time enough for the Martian to accomplish his purpose. And he, Ralph 124C 41 +, the greatest inventor the world had ever produced, was powerless.

Again he took observations, and again the results were the same. A weariness of the spirit swept over him. The dark waters of despair seemed to inundate his very soul. To have been physically exhausted would have been a relief. To know the blessedness of but an hour's sound sleep, to be free from this terrible tension—

He sank down upon a seat and buried his head in his hands, and as he sat, striving to quiet his worn and troubled mind there came to him an idea—nay, more than an idea, an inspiration, by which he would overcome the formidable difficulties that beset him.

An idea, so simple that, having once formulated it, it seemed ridiculous not to have thought of it before.

His soul-weariness fell from him like a discarded garment. He sprang to his feet, once more the scientist, the man of action, triumphant, dominant.

His marvelous ingenuity saw the way out. His mind would again triumph over time and space. He would achieve the impossible, surmount the insurmountable.

The battle was not lost—it had but begun!

He knew he could not overhaul Llysanorh'. Neither could he intercept him. A wireless decoy message was futile. Llysanorh' would never be caught by such a flimsy trick. But he must do something to prevent Llysanorh' from reaching Mars.

How could it be accomplished? By sending a message to the Martian authorities? A futile thought. Even if the distance could be bridged, which was doubtful, Llysanorh' would, in all likelihood, intercept the message with his recorder. He would simply send a message to his friend to board a space flyer and to rush to him at top speed. The marriage ceremony could then be performed out in space.

No, Llysanorh' must not know that he was pursued and still he must be prevented from landing.

Ralph would literally move the heavens. He would threaten Mars with a comet! Llysanorh's patriotism could be depended upon to make an effort to divert the comet from its course, to avoid the imminent collision with Mars.

This, Llysanorh' could do without danger to himself, simply by steering his flyer close to the head of the comet—within a few hundred kilometers. The gravitational action of his machine on the comet would deflect the course of the latter enough—even a few degrees would be sufficient to change the path of the meteor.

But where was the comet to come from? To Ralph this was simplicity itself. He did not need to "catch" a comet —*he would manufacture one for himself*—a comet more unique than ever rushed through space.

He knew that comets had been reproduced artificially on a small scale, centuries ago; * however, no one had

* In 1876 Reitlinger & Urbanitzky before the Vienna Academy of Sciences published a report on their experiments on artificial comets. A tube containing hydrocarbon has been pumped out till the pressure has fallen to 0.1 millimeter. If connected to an induction coil, a blue sphere will be formed at the positive electrode after a short time, which "hangs" suspended freely. Connected to the sphere is a tail, fig. 1. One is struck immediately with the close resemblance between this artificial comet and that of Henry's Comet of 1873, fig. 2. If a

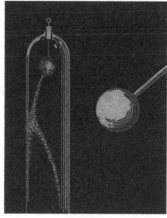

Fig. 1   Fig. 2

ever tried to make a real comet. He also knew that the largest comets have a very small mass, and that the tail is composed mainly of gas and dust, which is so thin that the stars may be readily observed through the tail of almost any comet.*

Ralph thus became the first human being to *create* a heavenly body. As comets are composed mainly of hydrogen gas and dust, the creating of Ralph's artificial comet was absurdly simple to the scientist.

By means of scraps of zinc and iron filings, over which sulphuric acid was poured, Ralph produced a great quantity of hydrogen. This he filled in tanks and when he had generated enough of the gas he connected the tanks with a large metal stop cock in the wall of the space flyer. As soon as the stop cock was opened the hydrogen rushed out into the open with a roar.

Immediately Ralph connected his high frequency apparatus with the outside aerials of the space flyer and the expected phenomenon took place.

---

conductor (a brass ball) as seen in fig. 1 is brought near the tube, the tail flees from the conductor as far as the tube allows. This again proves that the artificial as well as the real comets are subject to the same natural laws. As is known, the tails of all comets are repulsed strongly by the sun, which latter is nothing but a conductor.

* According to Bredikhine, the long straight tails, as seen in the comet of 1861, are composed of hydrogen; the long curved tails, like the principal tail of Donati's Comet, consist largely of hydrocarbon vapors; while the somnolent, rare, short tails of violent curvature are made up of mixed iron, sodium and other metallic vapors. This classification has received support from spectroscopic evidence. In 1882, Fitzgerald first propounded the theory that the tail was due to the pressure of light upon the gaseous matter composing it. In 1900 Arrhenius revived the theory, but modified it to the extent of supposing the tail to consist, not of gaseous matter, but of fine particles produced by condensation from the emanations of the comet.—New International Encyclopædia.

The hydrogen particles which heretofore had been invisible, began to glow with a wonderful light, enveloping the entire flyer. For thousands of miles behind the machine stretched a true comet's tail, the flyer forming its head or nucleus. The tail, as in all comets, was turned away from the sun, and although Ralph could not see the end of the tail, he knew that what he had created could be seen for hundreds of thousands of miles, like any natural comet.

Ralph, however, was not fully satisfied, and he therefore started to "improve" the comet. He manufactured several other gases in large quantities, which he ejected into space, greatly enhancing the brilliancy and size of the comet's head as well as of its tail.

The head, however, he thought was not "solid" enough as yet, and so he set about correcting this defect.

Comets are composed chiefly of gases, but contain a large amount of dust. The dust particles act very much like the dust particles upon which a sun ray falls, and it is these particles which create the comet's appearance. If the atmosphere is eliminated and the same dust placed into outer space, a small comet will result. The small particles will be highly electrified by the sun and begin to glow. Each particle repels the other and thus even a handful of light dust will form a respectable comet in space.

Ralph made his dust by grinding paper and wood and other materials on a fine carborundum wheel.

After he had made a few pails full, he blew the dust out into space, and if his comet had been a magnificent sight before, it was really awe-inspiring to look upon now from a great distance.

The heavier particles clung close to the flyer, on account of gravitational action, but completely enveloped it. The machine was now a true planet, while the fine dust particles had become little satellites, revolving around their central body, the flyer.

The lighter dust particles found their way into the tail, as the powerful pressure of the sun's light overcame the attraction which the flyer brought upon them.

Ralph turned off the high frequency current and yet the comet was not extinguished and its brilliance was not in the least dimmed. The gas and dust particles had no way to dissipate their initial electrical charge, being in an absolute vacuum; and Ralph's artificial comet had become a real one.

Inasmuch as the dust was quite dense immediately around the flyer, Ralph's outlook was not as clear as it had been before. He could just see the stars, which seemed enveloped in a haze. This, however, pleased him greatly, as he knew that his artificial comet must look like a natural one from a great distance.

In this he had not been mistaken. As he afterwards learned, his comet had been "discovered" simultaneously on Earth, on Venus, and on Mars the same day he had made it. It had been charted and named, and on account of its great brilliance and long tail, had been immediately termed "The Great Comet of 2660."

That Llysanorh' would see the comet Ralph never doubted for a second. He headed his comet-space flyer exactly toward the point where it would collide with Mars at the end of six days. He figured that the Martians would be on the lookout, and inasmuch as Ralph's careful search did not reveal another space flyer anywhere near him, he knew that the Martian officials would surely locate and attempt to communicate with Llysanorh'.

In this he was not mistaken. His chronometer pointed to 5 p. m. when he first recorded weak signals coming from Mars. Several messages were exchanged between the Martians and Llysanorh'. Llysanorh' gave his number and position in the heavens and he in turn received instructions to approach as near to the "comet's" head as feasible in order to change its course. He was also instructed to bombard the comet's nucleus with time-set torpedoes, if he could not deviate the comet from its course. Llysanorh' answered that he would follow instructions as far as his equipment allowed.

During the next few days Ralph was relieved to note that the distance between him and Llysanorh' diminished with great rapidity. His trick had worked. Llysanorh' was rushing at top speed toward Ralph's flyer, firmly believing it a comet.

Confident of success, sure of victory, Ralph was jubilant. Hope, so long deferred, flooded his spirit. He whistled cheerily at his work.

Was not every minute bringing him closer to his sweetheart, his Alice? Was not every second drawing nearer to that moment when he would hold her in his arms?

What wonder that he whistled all day long, and laughed to himself from sheer joy and relief.

At last the Martian came into range. Llysanorh' approached the "comet" up to about 150 kilometers and then receded. He then took observations, but somehow or other the "comet," instead of being deflected, commenced to pursue him. This was opposed to all astronomical knowledge and reasoning, and Llysanorh', fearing collision with the "comet" began to fire explosive

183

torpedoes into its nucleus. As the distance between it and his machine was only 100 kilometers, he could watch the torpedo in its flight. Through his telescope he could see the torpedo rushing toward the "comet's" head.

But the "comet" dodged, and the torpedo shot far above the nucleus! It was uncanny. His aim had been accurate, he could have sworn. The distance was short. Yet he had missed. The "comet" had moved out of the projectile's path.

He had fired again, with equal accuracy. The torpedo would surely strike now. But the "comet" this time "sidestepped," as it were, and the torpedo sped on through space, missing its target by a wide margin.

Llysanorh' was bewildered. Fear gripped him.

Gravitational action had not made the "comet" act in this strange manner. He fired one torpedo after another, but the "comet" dodged them all.

He suddenly stopped firing torpedoes. He next tried to destroy the infernal "comet" by electricity.

Soon his aerials were white hot with the energy he threw into them. He then turned his flyer into such a position as to direct the outflowing energy towards the "comet's" head. The only result was to increase the luminosity of the "comet."

Suddenly Llysanorh' realized that the "comet" was only fifty kilometers away. He noticed with horror that the head of the "comet" now seemed to fill up almost one-quarter of the "sky." Another discovery that came simultaneously was that instead of the "comet's" head being solid, there was a mysterious small black speck in the center of the nucleus. This was against both knowledge and theory of comets.

When Ralph had brought his "comet" within fifty kilometers of Llysanorh', he felt that the time had come to throw off the mask. He had lured Llysanorh' to within striking distance. It was now time to strike.

He had one great advantage over Llysanorh'. The latter was wholly unprepared, believing he had to deal with a comet. This facilitated Ralph's movements.

He carefuly insulated himself by sitting on a tall glass tripod. He then attached to his ears the telephone receivers that were connected with the induction balance,* which he had attached to one of the glass port-holes.

He then started to turn the glass wheel of the ultra-generator, connected to the outside aerials.

A terrible screaming sound came from the generator and the whole flyer shook. Ralph continued to turn the wheel quickly. The generator shrilled higher and higher, until the frequency had become so high that no sound could be heard. The vibrations had passed 35,000.

Ralph turned the wheel a few more notches and everything became pitch-dark over a space sixty kilometers in diameter.

As in his Switzerland exploit, two months before, Ralph's aerial on the space flyer due to the powerful action of his ultra-generator, attracted the ether so fast that it could not be replenished quickly enough. It acted much like an immense vacuum pump on the atmosphere.

Darkness spread over a large area as the inky fluid of

* The induction balance is an instrument which, connected with a telephone, causes the latter to emit a singing sound, when a piece of metal is brought near the balance. It is incredibly sensitive and has been used to locate buried treasures, etc. Invented in 1880 by Professor Hughes.

the octopus blackens the sea. Both flyers became invisible to each other.

Ralph, however, pointed his machine on its former course and speeded it up.

Llysanorh', dismayed by the unexpected darkness, had brought his machine to a dead stop. He was almost frantic with terror and stood like one paralyzed, unable to think or to act.

Within a few minutes Ralph's induction balance caused his telephones to emit higher and higher notes, indicating, despite the pitch-black darkness, just how near he was to the other flyer.

When he was certain that he had approached Llysanorh's machine, he suddenly shut off his ultra-generator. Quick as lightning he had grasped his radioperforer, and although the light which returned instantly blinded him for a few seconds, he had glimpsed Llysanorh's terrified face, just a few meters distant, his forehead pressed tight against the glass plate of the port-hole.

Ralph took quick aim and pressed the trigger.

There was a silent flash and Llysanorh' seemed to topple over. Simultaneously the glass of the port-hole turned green.

In a flash Ralph jumped up and peered anxiously out one port-hole, then another, hoping to catch sight of Alice.

There was nobody to be seen.

He rushed to the wireless and signaled frantically for several minutes. Breathlessly he clasped the receivers to his ears.

There was no answer—no sound—nothing.

With sinking heart, he rushed to the connecting tube.

In his excitement it took him twenty minutes to make the connection between the two machines and the tube airtight. Before crawling into the connecting tube he grabbed up his radioperforer as a precaution.

The sight that presented itself to him as he crawled into Llysanorh's machine drew from him an involuntary agonized cry.

Llysanorh's dead body lay across that of Alice, his sharp dagger sunk into the upper part of her arm. Ralph hurriedly moved the rigid body aside.

There lay Alice in a terrible pool of her own blood, her eyes closed—dead.

15

LLYSANORH' THROWS OFF THE MASK

WHEN ALICE SAW that it was Llysanorh' standing on the threshold of her room she experienced at once great disappointment and overwhelming relief.

The second space flyer was not driven by Ralph, but she was at least safe from Fernand.

"Oh," she cried with a sob of relief, "I am so glad it is you, Llysanorh'! I have been so frightened."

He made no answer, but regarded her with enormous eyes in which burned a somber flame.

"You *are* going to take me off this horrible flyer, aren't you, Llysanorh'? You won't leave me here alone with that —that beast, will you?"

He shook his head soberly, and extended one hand to her.

"Come," he said briefly.

She put her own hand confidently in his, and he led her down the stairs, and past the laboratory. She shrank back as she saw Fernand's bound and motionless form.

"Is he—dead?" she whispered.

"No," said Llysanorh', leading her to the connecting tube. He helped her through with gentle hands, and in a moment she found herself in the other flyer. Taking her hand again in his, Llysanorh' led her to a luxuriously furnished room.

"Stay here until I come back," he said. "I won't be long."

He turned to go but she, catching his sleeve, detained him.

"Are you going to—to kill him?" she asked.

"Perhaps. I haven't decided yet," he replied, unsmiling. And then, gripping her shoulders with startlingly sudden emotion, "Has he harmed you?"

"No, no," she said, frightened, "he just tried to terrify me, that was all."

He released her, and strode to the door.

"I won't kill him," he said, and for the first time he smiled, but in that smile there was no mirth. "I shall let him live, that he may pray for the death I have denied him."

And he was gone.

Presently Alice heard him disconnecting the two machines, and a moment later she knew that Llysanorh's flyer was moving. A half hour passed and still she was left alone. Beyond the vibration of the machinery there was no sound to indicate that she was not absolutely alone on the flyer.

Feeling a little panicky she finally left the room and made her way through a corridor. Several doors that she opened led into rooms even more luxurious and splendid than the one she had left.

So this was the space flyer owned by the Martian of which there had been so much gossip. Stories she had heard before of its spaciousness and magnificence came back to her.

It was like the palace of the Beast in the ancient fairy story, where Beauty had wandered for hours through room after room filled with new marvels. Alice smiled whimsically at the thought. She was "Beauty," she reflected, and Llysanorh'—yes, he made a very good "Beast." Her buoyant spirits were rapidly recovering from the strain of her imprisonment.

Finally, she tried one more door, and entered a wonderful laboratory fully equipped.

And at the farther end, seated before a low table sat the Martian, his head resting on his folded arms. His whole attitude suggested hopeless desolation. He looked very lonely and remote, and somehow, to her, very pathetic.

She stood, hesitating, uncertain of whether to advance or retreat. Finally she spoke his name softly. At her voice he raised his head and stared at her. And she saw that his face was lined and furrowed as if with some terrible strain, but his eyes were steady with resolve.

"How serious you look," she said, coming into the middle of the room. "You seem so worried and anxious, Llysanorh'. Has something gone wrong with the flyer? And what did you do with Fernand and his machine?"

"I left him recovering from the effects of the drug," he said, in a forced and unnatural voice which betrayed, even more than his expression, the disturbed state of his mind. "And nothing is wrong with the flyer. It is I—I with whom everything is wrong."

"Oh, surely it can't be as bad as you think," said the girl, her quick sympathies aroused by his obvious misery. "Would it make you feel any better to tell me? We have always been such good friends. Llysanorh', and I might be able to help you."

"Later, perhaps, later," he said, and then with an effort, "can you make yourself comfortable here for a few days,

190

do you think? I brought the maid with me. You will find her waiting in your rooms for you. I don't think she will give you any trouble."

"Oh, yes, I surely can," she replied. "It is lovely here. I have heard so much of this flyer. Why haven't you shown it to father and me before? The rooms are like those of a fairy palace. Tell me Llysanorh', will it be long before we get back to Earth? Everyone"—she had been about to say Ralph, but checked herself—"everyone will be so worried about me."

"We are never going back to Earth," he said.

"Never going—why, what has happened then? Is there something wrong that you won't tell me?—or are you joking? But of course you're joking, Llysanorh', and for a minute I thought you were serious."

"I was never more serious," he said, rising to his feet and facing her. "We are never going back, you and I."

Alice looked at him wide-eyed, amazed and bewildered.

"But I don't undersand," she faltered. "Why, Llysanorh'?"

It was then that the pent-up emotion of months burst the bonds of self-restraint that he had forced upon himself.

"Why!" he cried passionately, "you ask me why! Can't you see why? How can you look into my eyes and not know why? Because I am a man—because I am a fool—good God, because I love you!" He flung himself upon his knees, clasping her about the waist with his arms.

"I worship you, I adore you—I always shall. You must love me, you cannot help but love me, I love you so much, Alice, Alice, my dearest, my beloved."

He threw his head back and looked into her face im-

191

ploringly, as if by the very force of his love she must respond, but he read there only terror and a growing abhorrence. It cooled him more effectually than any words she could have spoken, and he relinquished his hold on her, rose and went back to his former position at the table, while she watched him speechlessly.

For a time neither spoke. At last he said in quiet tones strangely in contrast with his late passion, "You can't hate me, Alice, I love you too much."

"No," she said, gently, "I don't hate you, Llysanorh', but oh, can't you see how hopeless all this is? I love Ralph, and if you keep me here forever I will still love him."

She got a glimpse, then, of the terrible struggle this man of Mars had had with his conscience.

"I know, I know," he groaned, "I have gone over that ground many times—many times, but I can not—will not —give you up. I tell you," he went on with a return of his former frenzied emotion, "that rather than let him have you I will kill you with my own hands. At least, when you are dead I will be sure that no other man can possess you."

She was a courageous girl, but before the madness in his face she fled shuddering.

During the next several days Alice kept close to her rooms. She saw little of Llysanorh', who seemed to be avoiding her purposely, and the maid, Lylette, was uncommunicative. Alice was horribly lonely and afraid. At first she had confidently expected Ralph to rescue her at any moment, but as the days dragged on, and still the space flyer drew nearer to Mars, and there were no signs of Ralph, she became increasingly aware that her situation was desperate.

She knew that Llysanorh' controlled powerful interests on his native planet, and that once there, all her pleadings would be in vain and he would make her his bride.

The few times she saw him he was quiet in manner, showing a courteous deference to her. But he could not hide the triumphant light in his eyes, which, the nearer they came to Mars, he took less pains to disguise from her. And yet, she could not deny the fact of his genuine, and fervent love for her. Only once, did he again speak of it.

One day she was sitting in the beautifully appointed library reading, with Lylette near by, when he entered. He gazed at her a moment in silence. Then he said, "You know, Alice, just to have you here with me, where I can see you occasionally, is wonderful to me."

Her eyes filled with quick tears, for she was worn and unhappy. And seeing them he quickly withdrew.

Later, he seemed very busy in the machine room. Passing it, once, she saw him working frantically at something; what, she could not see. But a glimpse of his face revealed it haggard and drawn. It was but a few minutes after that, back in her own room, a complete and terrifying blackness obliterated everything. She heard Lylette screaming somewhere in dreadful panic, and she heard Llysanorh' shout something hoarsely.

Stumbling, she made her way as fast as she could in the darkness back to the machine room. She heard him at one of the windows. Apparently he was trying to pierce the blackness, to ascertain its cause. She started toward him, when the light returned in a blinding flash, and she saw

Llysanorh' stagger as if struck by something.

"Llysanorh'," she cried, "what is it? What is happening?"

He lurched toward her and caught her in his arms savagely. "I'll tell you what has happened," he shouted, "I see it all now. The comet—a trick, damn him! And now he's got me. But not you, Alice, not you. You are going with me—"

The Martian's face was distorted with passion. He had a gleaming dagger in his right hand poised over her. Then, just as it was about to strike she saw his face go blank and felt a terrific blow on her arm. The next instant she was slumping—seemed to drop off into a dreamless sleep.

16

THE SUPREME VICTORY

WHEN RALPH BURST into the machine room of the Martian's flyer and saw Alice lying dead in a pool of her own blood the shock was almost more than he could bear. Falling on his knees beside her he caught her small, yet warm hand in his, calling her name again and again in agonized tones. He covered her lovely white face with kisses, while dry tearless sobs tore at his throat.

Then, thinking that perhaps he had made a mistake, that her heart *must* still beat, he tried, with trembling hands to discover the extent of her injuries. Llysanorh' had aimed at her heart but the dying man had missed his mark, and the sharp point of the dagger had slashed her arm, cutting into the large artery. And in those precious moments when Ralph had been connecting the two flyers, and making his way from one to the other, her warm rich life's blood had ebbed rapidly away

He lifted the lifeless body in his arms and carried it to his machine, where he laid it on his bed. His mind was confused and disordered and he was unable to think coherently. A sickening sensation of depression so overwhelmed him that he felt physically ill.

Suddenly an electric thrill seemed to pass through his body and his clouded mental vision cleared. A picture flashed upon his mind. He saw himself in his laboratory on Earth, bending over a "dead" dog. And there came to him a memory of the words of that Dean of scientists:

"What you have done with a dog, you can do with a human being."

In that instant Ralph was galvanized. For the first time in his life he doubted. Could he do it? What if he failed? Then he pushed such thoughts from him with stern resolution.

He would not fail!

He touched the body of the girl. It had not yet grown cold with the icy chill of death. He rushed for some electric heating pads, which he applied to her to keep what warmth remained.

Then came that which proved itself a terrible ordeal for him. It was absolutely necessary to drain away all the remaining blood, so that it would not coagulate.

It had been a simple matter to empty the blood vessels of a dog, but this was the girl he loved, and he shuddered as he began his work.

He opened the large artery, and it was only with supreme courage that he forced himself to complete the heartbreaking task, while scalding tears ran down his cheeks unheeded.

He had scarcely terminated his work, when he heard steps in the corridor. He could feel his hair bristling, and he whirled to face the door, reaching for his radioperforer as he did so. Could Llysanorh'? . . . The next moment a large woman stood in the doorway.

Ralph stared at her in amazement. Then suddenly it dawned upon him that this must be the maid Fernand had provided.

She had hidden herself in abject terror when the darkness came down, and had only now mustered enough courage to investigate. The first object she had seen upon creeping to the machine room was the dead body of the Martian. Horrified, she had fainted away, but later, recovering, she crawled through the connecting tube.

She was weak, trembling with fright, and could be of no use, and Ralph hastened to get her into another room, where he put her into a comfortable chair and left her, for he could not afford to lose a minute now.

A most important task was now before him. He had to pump an antiseptic solution through the veins of Alice, and after that the blood vessels must be filled with a weak solution of Radium-K Bromide, which, taking the place of the blood would prevent her body from undergoing physical and chemical changes.

With infinite care Ralph applied himself to his difficult task. After the blood vessels had been completely filled with the Radium preparation, he sewed up the arteries. In this gruesome task he was assisted by Lylette, who had recovered sufficiently to be of some help to him.

There remained only one more thing—to apply the Permagatol, the rare gas, having the property of conserving animal tissue, which Ralph had used successfully in his dog experiment, in keeping the respiratory organs from decomposing in the absence of blood in the blood vessels.

Ralph then quickly constructed a case of flexible glass, which he fitted around the upper part of Alice's body, covering her head and torso.

He took special precautions, moreover, to make the case air-tight.

When the case had been completed and the recording

and registering instruments put in place, Ralph went up to the laboratory to get the Permagatol.

When, however, he tested the steelonium bomb, labeled "Permagatol," he found it absolutely empty.

The discovery nearly paralyzed him. His head swam and he was forced to sit down to keep from slumping over in the gravitation-less flyer. This last blow was almost too much. His cup of hope, that Alice could be brought back to life, had been snatched out of his hands.

Without the Permagatol, it was impossible to save her. There was nothing to keep the beautiful dead body from disintegrating. While the Radium-K Bromide stayed the process to a certain extent, the respiratory organs could only be saved by means of the precious Permagatol.

Could he use a substitute gas? It was a dangerous experiment to make, but he had nothing to lose, and everything to gain.

He threw himself with a frenzy into the work and in six hours had compounded a gas that, in its general structure and atomic weight, came close to the properties and characteristics of Permagatol. The gas he evolved was Armagatol, and while he knew that it had never been used for the purpose for which he intended it, he felt justified in risking the experiment.

After the air had been drawn from the glass case, he immediately introduced the Armagatol into it.

The change in Alice's face shocked him, as he watched the Armagatol fill the case. The green gas-vapors cast an unearthly green pallor over her countenance, and the ghastliness was further enhanced by the deathly pallor of her face.

He arranged the electric heating pads around Alice's

body, and inspected the registering instruments.

It had now become necessary to take his bearings. He found to his amazement that instead of being close to Mars, as he had expected, he was moving away from that body.

The two space flyers, although their machinery was not working, had been moving rapidly, due to the gravitational action of the nearest large celestial body. This body was not Mars, however, but Earth. Although, at the time of the encounter with Llysanorh', the two machines had been slightly nearer to Mars, the larger mass, and consequently the stronger attraction of the Earth had overcome the pull that Mars exerted on the machines, and as a result the machines were now being drawn toward Earth.

A glance at the celestial chart revealed to Ralph that Earth and Mars would be in opposition the next day and that he was separated from Earth by twenty-two million miles. He would have to move faster than Earth if he were to overtake that body. Besides, he was twenty-two million miles to the east of the planet.

The Earth was traveling 65,533 miles per hour in its orbit. A simple calculation indicated that, by forcing his space flyer to the utmost, or 90,000 miles an hour, he could not hope to reach Earth in less than fifty days, as he could only gain about 24,400 miles an hour on Earth.

The next important step was to cut loose Llysanorh's machine. He instructed Lylette to get her things from the Martian's flyer. She started to crawl through the connecting tube, and that was the last time Ralph saw her alive.

A loud hissing noise, like escaping steam caused him to rush to the connecting tube, but he was too late. The automatic safety valve had sprung, and the circular door of the connecting tube had been hermetically closed.

The two machines had drifted apart, and as Ralph peered anxiously through one of the windows, he was horrified at the sight of Lylette, hanging by her feet from the circular connecting-tube door of Llysanorh's machine.

The door had closed automatically when the two machines had become disconnected. The air had of course rushed out immediately from Llysanorh's flyer. She had died in a few seconds and her body had become distended to a great many times its normal size. Ralph, nauseated by the terrible spectacle, turned away from it. There was nothing he could do.

Few people realize that it is nothing but the atmospheric pressure that keeps our bodies from falling apart; thus, it is well known that when flying at high altitudes on the Earth, where the atmosphere becomes thin, blood will begin to flow from the mouth, nose and ears.

When he glanced backwards a few minutes later and saw Llysanorh's machine he gave an exclamation of astonishment. The machine was not to be seen, but in its place was a wondrous comet, its tail streaming thousands of miles behind it!

Llysanorh's flyer, which was somewhat larger in size than that of Ralph's, had "captured" the artificial comet! There remained not a part of it attached to Ralph's flyer. Ralph reasoned that the air that had been contained formerly in Llysanorh's machine had, upon rushing out of the flyer after Lylette's fatal accident, mixed with the gases of the "comet" and thereby assisted the latter in detaching itself from Ralph's flyer.

It remained within range of his vision for many weeks,

before it was finally lost in the depths of infinite space, where it would, in all probability, rush through the boundless universe for aeon upon aeon, ere it would eventually collide with some other body, and would be reduced to cosmic dust.

The long days during Ralph's flight back to Earth left their indelible imprint upon his mind. Never, in all the years to follow, could he look back upon them without a shudder, remembering the heart-break of the terrible hours in which he sat beside the bed on which lay his beloved.

The nearer he drew to Earth, the more his dread of the coming ordeal increased. He was by no means sure that he could bring Alice back to life; it was not even probable. It was but an experiment at best, the outcome of which could not be foretold. If Armagatol would bring the same reactions as Permagatol, there was a reasonable assurance of restoring Alice to life, but Ralph was inclined to doubt the efficiency of the substitute gas.

He examined her every few hours, and once in twenty-four he looked at the blood vessels. This was made possible by means of his *Platinum-Barium-Arcturium* eyeglasses, which acted in a similar manner to the old-fashioned X-ray screen. Inasmuch as all the blood vessels of Alice's body were filled with Radium-K Bromide—which latter, like Radium, excited the Platinum-Barium-Arcturium eyeglasses—each blood vessel could be inspected with ease.

The invisible Rays (the same as X-rays) emanating from the Radium-K Bromide solution in the blood vessels, showed Ralph their exact condition.

While all the blood vessels remained healthy, Ralph became greatly alarmed over the change that slowly, but steadily, made itself apparent in the respiratory organs. Some change was taking place which he did not understand. He knew it must be the action of the Armagatol, but he was unable to do anything, as with the chemicals on hand it was impossible to produce the life-saving Permagatol.

Ralph grew more despondent each day, and his hope of bringing his betrothed back to life grew dimmer and dimmer as the hours rolled on. For the first time since he left the Earth he became *space-sick.*

Space-sickness is one of the most unpleasant sensations that a human being can experience. Not all are subject to it, and it does not last longer than forty-eight hours, after which it never recurs.

On Earth, gravitational action to a certain degree exerts a certain pull on the brain. Out in space, with practically no gravitational action, this pull ceases. When this happens, the brain is no longer subjected to the accustomed pull, and it expands slightly in all directions, just as a balloon loses its pear shape and becomes round when an aeronaut cuts loose, to drop down with his parachute.

The effect on the brain results in space-sickness, the first symptoms being violent melancholy and depression followed by a terrible heart-rending longing for Earth. During this stage, at which the patient undergoes great mental suffering, the optical nerves usually become affected and everything appears upside down, as if the sufferer were looking through a lens. It becomes necessary to take large doses of *Siltagol,* otherwise brain fever may develop.

At the end of two days the sickness left Ralph, but it left him worn and exhausted physically and he was subject to terrible fits of depression. At these times the boundless space about him appalled him, weighing him down with its infinite immensity. The awful stillness crushed him. Everything seemed dead—dead as was that silent motionless figure that had been a living laughing creature who had loved him—it seemed so long ago.

He felt that Nature herself was punishing him for his daring assault upon her dominions. He had presumed to set the laws of Life and Death at variance, and this was the penalty, this living death, shut in with the living dead.

At such times a madness of fear and despair would grip him. He would fling himself down at Alice's side, his face buried in her cold inert hand, and sob like a child in his loneliness and agony of spirit.

When this had passed he would return to his state of lethargy, sitting hours at a time staring moodily at the floor. Gaunt, hollow-eyed and listless, he seemed more mad than sane.

And yet, the tremendous will-power of the man came into evidence when, within forty-eight hours' distance of Earth he threw off his blinding lethargy, and made himself ready, mentally and physically, for his last fight for Alice's life.

He had drawn close enough to Earth now to use the Radio apparatus, and soon he was in hourly communication with his laboratory. He gave his instructions clearly and definitely, and he soon had assurance that everything that could possibly be done for the dead girl had been carefully arranged.

Ralph's flyer landed on top of his tower sixty-nine days

after his departure. He was greatly impressed at the sight of the flags of the city at half mast. The town itself was very still. There were no aeroflyers, no vehicles in motion in the streets. Business was at a standstill for ten minutes after Ralph landed. Thus the world expressed its deep sympathy.

Within a few minutes Alice had been placed on an operating table in Ralph's laboratory, and 16K 5 +, the world's greatest surgeon, who had been summoned, was in readiness. Ralph was placed on an operating table to the right of Alice. To the left lay Cléose, a beloved cousin of Alice.

In a few seconds Alice's arteries had been opened and the Radium-K Bromide solution was drawn off. A quantity of warm, distilled water, containing antiseptic salts was then pumped through her blood vessels by two assistants. During this time the surgeon had opened the large arteries of both Ralph and Cléose, and had introduced a flexible glass tube into each. In a short time the blood of Ralph and Cléose began flowing rapidly through these tubes into Alice's blood vessels.

Simultaneously a third assistant administered oxygen to Alice, while a fourth commenced to excite her heart rhythmically by means of electrical current.

The brain was stimulated energetically at the same time by means of the powerful F-9-Rays, and while Ralph and Cléose grew paler and paler as their blood flowed out into Alice's body, the latter began to acquire color by degrees, though there was no other sign of life. After enough blood had been taken from the two, the surgeon closed their arteries; and, while Cléose had fainted during the ordeal,

Ralph, weakened as he was, remained conscious by sheer force of will.

The surgeon 16K 5 +, asked Ralph if he did not think it would be better for him to be removed to another room, but Ralph refused so vehemently, despite his terribly depleted strength, that he was allowed to remain. He asked to be raised slightly higher that he might watch the work of restoring Alice to life, and this request too, was granted.

Almost two hours had passed since Alice had first been laid upon the operating table, and still there was no sign of life. The suspense became well-nigh unendurable, not only to Ralph, but to the workers as well.

Was she lost after all?

Was he fated never to see her alive again?

The great surgeon and his assistants were working desperately. Every conceivable means was used to revive the inanimate body, but all was to no avail. As attempt after attempt failed the faces of the men grew graver. A tense silence prevailed throughout the laboratory, broken only by the surgeon's sharp low instructions from time to time.

It was then, when the tide of hope was at the lowest ebb, that Ralph beckoned one of the assistants to his side. Though unable to speak above a whisper, so weak was he, he managed with difficulty to convey his meaning to the man, who sprang to the side of the surgeon and in a low voice gave him Ralph's message.

Ralph had sent for a Hypnobioscope, the head pieces of which they fastened to Alice's temples. They brought a number of rolls and from them Ralph chose one of the world's most beautiful love stories.

It was the last trench in his desperate combat with Nature. It was the supreme effort. It was the last throw of the dice in the game between Science and Death, with a girl as the stakes.

Ralph knew that if the brain was at all alive to impressions, the effect of the story would stimulate it to voluntary action.

As the reel unrolled, Ralph fixed his burning eyes on the closed ones as though he would drive by the very force of his will the impressions coming from the Hypnobioscope deep into her brain.

Then, while they watched, with bated breath, the slight body on the operating table quivered almost imperceptibly, as the water of a still pool is rippled by a passing zephyr. A moment later her breast rose gently and fell again, and from the white lips came the suggestion of a sigh.

When Ralph saw this, his strength returned to him, and he raised himself, listening with throbbing heart to the soft breathing. His eyes glowed with triumph. The battle was won. His face was transfigured. All the agony, the heart-breaking foreboding of the past weeks passed from him, and a great peace settled upon his soul.

The surgeon sprang to catch him as he dropped, unconscious.

About a week later Ralph was admitted by the nurse to the room where Alice lay, regaining her strength. He was still weak, himself, from the loss of blood. Alice had just awakened, and at his step, she turned her lovely face eagerly toward him. Her cheeks were faintly tinged with the delicate pink of the seashell, her eyes were bright with the soft glow of health.

She beckoned to him smiling into his eyes, and he knelt down beside her, taking her hands in his own, and holding them close. She moved her lips and he bent his head close to them, so that her gentle breath fanned his cheek.

"I can't talk very loud," she whispered. "My lungs and vocal chords are not strong yet, but the nurse said I might speak just a few words. But I wanted to tell you something."

"What is it, my darling?" he asked tenderly.

She looked at him with the old sparkle of mischief in her dark eyes.

"Dearest," she said, "I have just found out what your name really means."

Ralph twined a little tendril of her hair around one of his fingers.

"Yes?" he asked with a quizzical smile.

"Well, you see," and the lovely color deepened to rose, "your name is going to be my name now, so I keep saying it over to myself—"

"My darling
ONE TO FORESEE FOR ONE!"
(1   2   4   C   4   1)

CPSIA information can be obtained
at www.ICGtesting.com
Printed in the USA
LVHW091534231218
601536LV00006B/650/P